The Clockmaker's Secret Gift

Freya Jobe

Published by Freya Jobe, 2024.

This is a work of fiction. Similarities to real people, places, or events are entirely coincidental.

THE CLOCKMAKER'S SECRET GIFT

First edition. November 6, 2024.

Copyright © 2024 Freya Jobe.

ISBN: 979-8227869838

Written by Freya Jobe.

The Clockmaker's Secret Gift
A magical clockmaker gives a broken clock to a family that can make time slow down.

Once upon a time, in a bustling little town filled with hurrying people and ticking clocks, there was a tiny shop tucked away on a quiet, winding street. It was the kind of place most folks passed by without even noticing. But to those who did see it, the shop looked as if it were from another time altogether, with its brass doorknob polished to a gleam and a delicate sign swinging above that read, Tockman's Clocks: Timepieces and Wonders.

Inside the shop was a peculiar old man named Mr. Tockman, who spent his days fixing all kinds of clocks—tall, wooden grandfather clocks with booming chimes, pocket watches with ticking hearts, and even the odd wristwatch that needed a new spring. But what few people knew was that Mr. Tockman wasn't just a regular clockmaker. His clocks held secrets, and, if he thought you were the right person, he might share a bit of their magic with you.

One cold autumn evening, as the sun dipped below the rooftops and painted the sky in warm, rosy hues, a small family hurried by his shop. The father had papers tucked under his arm, the mother balanced bags in both hands, and the two children skipped along, their laughter bouncing off the cobblestone street. They didn't know it then, but they were about to discover the secret that Mr. Tockman had been waiting years to share.

And so begins the story of a very special gift—a broken clock that could slow down time itself. It's the tale of what happens when a family learns how to pause the rush of life, to savour each other's laughter, and to find the magic in every precious moment.

Little did they know, the magic of that gift wasn't just in slowing down the world around them, but in discovering the wonders within their own hearts.

Part 1: The Clockmaker's Gift
Chapter 1: The Little Clock Shop

The town was alive with its usual morning rush. Street vendors set up carts, buskers tuned their instruments, and the bakery on the corner filled the air with the scent of freshly baked bread and cinnamon rolls. Down the main street, nestled between a bookshop and a small cafe, stood a peculiar little store that few people seemed to notice. Its sign, delicately painted in gold letters, read: Tockman's Clocks: Timepieces and Wonders.

The shop was small, with faded green paint on the door and a large window filled with an assortment of clocks of every shape and size. Some were elegant, carved from dark mahogany, and others were quirky, painted in bright colors with faces that almost seemed to smile. From cuckoo clocks to stately grandfather clocks, each piece seemed to have a personality, as though they were waiting for someone special to come along and listen to their unique ticking.

Most people hurried past without a glance, too busy with their own lives to notice. But the Baxter family—Mr. and Mrs. Baxter and their two children, Emma and Max—always took an extra moment to look. Every weekday morning, as they walked to school and work, they passed by Tockman's Clocks, each of them drawn to it in their own way.

Seven-year-old Emma was especially fascinated by the shop. She had curly red hair and wide blue eyes that noticed every little detail. She loved books, especially stories about magic and adventure, and she couldn't help but wonder if Tockman's Clocks might be the setting of one of her tales. She imagined that each clock in the window had a secret—maybe one could make time go backward, or another could make you invisible.

"Do you think the clocks are magical, Mom?" she asked, tugging on her mother's hand as they strolled past the shop.

Mrs. Baxter chuckled, glancing down at her daughter. "Oh, Emma, you have such a wonderful imagination. But I think they're just regular clocks—beautiful, yes, but no more magical than the ones at home."

"But look, Mom!" Emma insisted, pointing to a large clock in the window with gold trim and silver hands. "That one glows a little! Can you see it?"

Mrs. Baxter squinted at the clock, noticing nothing out of the ordinary, but she smiled and nodded. "Maybe it's a trick of the light," she said, although she felt a small, unusual pull from the shop herself.

Emma's ten-year-old brother, Max, was just as curious, though in a quieter way. Max loved puzzles and figuring out how things worked. Every morning, he pressed his face against the shop's glass window, trying to get a glimpse of the insides of the clocks, curious about how the gears and springs moved together to make such steady ticking sounds.

"I bet I could take one of those clocks apart and put it back together," Max mused to his father one morning, glancing sideways at a peculiar clock that had no numbers on it, just dots in odd places. "I wonder if Mr. Tockman would let me look inside one."

Mr. Baxter laughed, ruffling Max's hair. "Knowing you, Max, you'd figure out its secrets in no time. But maybe it's better to leave these clocks alone. They seem... well, special."

Max nodded, but his eyes lingered on the shop, hoping that one day he'd get to see the inside of one of those unusual clocks. He'd heard of Mr. Tockman, the clockmaker, but hadn't ever seen him up close. People around town said he was a bit of a mystery—quiet, rarely seen outside the shop, and always surrounded by ticking clocks.

And, indeed, Tockman's Clocks had a reputation. People who did venture inside said it was unlike any other shop in town. They described Mr. Tockman as an older man with a bushy mustache and round glasses that magnified his kind, twinkling eyes. He was always dressed in a neat vest with a pocket watch tucked inside, and he had a way of speaking that made people feel like they'd known him for years. But what people remembered most was the feeling of calm that washed over them when they left the shop, as though time had slowed down, just for a moment.

As they passed the shop one brisk autumn morning, Max noticed something unusual. The shop's window was open just a crack, and he could faintly hear the ticking of all the clocks inside. The sound was strangely calming, each tick blending with the others into a kind of gentle music. Max stopped, tilting his head to listen.

"Do you hear that, Mom?" he asked, his voice barely a whisper.

Mrs. Baxter paused, closing her eyes for a moment as the ticking sounds filled the cool morning air. She could hear it, too—a soft, rhythmic ticking that almost felt like it was matching her heartbeat.

"It's... lovely," she murmured, surprised at how comforting the sound was.

Emma leaned closer to the window, squinting inside. "Do you think Mr. Tockman ever leaves his shop?" she asked. "I never see him anywhere else."

Mr. Baxter chuckled, checking his watch. "He's probably inside fixing clocks all day. I've heard he's a bit of a night owl, working late into the night to keep the town's clocks in perfect time."

Emma's eyes widened. "Maybe he's a wizard! He could be fixing more than clocks. Maybe he can fix time itself."

Max raised an eyebrow. "Time isn't broken, Emma."

She crossed her arms, undeterred. "How do you know? Maybe it is, and we just don't realize it because he's been keeping it fixed this whole time!"

"Alright, you two," Mrs. Baxter said, stifling a laugh. "We'd better get going. You don't want to be late for school."

But even as they walked away, Emma's gaze lingered on the shop. She could feel something strange about it, something unexplainable that left a spark of excitement inside her.

Over the next few days, she and Max became even more captivated by the little shop. Each day, the window display seemed to shift. One morning, it featured an old-fashioned cuckoo clock with a bird that peeked out every few seconds, as though it were watching them. Another day, the clocks were arranged to look like the face of a giant owl, with two clocks as eyes and a row of tiny silver pocket watches as its feathers. The next day, a set of hourglasses appeared, filled with sand that glittered as it slipped from one half to the other, catching the morning light.

Mr. and Mrs. Baxter couldn't help but notice their children's fascination. They exchanged glances, silently agreeing that maybe, one of these days, they would let the children step inside and explore. It seemed like such a small thing, yet each time they passed the shop, the idea of entering felt like an adventure waiting to happen.

Then, one evening, as the family walked home together in the fading light, they noticed something strange. The clock shop was still open. The golden glow from inside spilled out onto the street, painting the cobblestones with a warm, inviting light. The door was slightly ajar, and from within came the faint sounds of ticking and a gentle humming that sounded almost like a lullaby.

Emma stopped in her tracks, her eyes shining with excitement. "Mom, Dad, the shop is open! Can we go inside?"

Mrs. Baxter hesitated, glancing at Mr. Baxter. She couldn't deny the shop's pull—it seemed to invite them in, almost as if it were expecting them. But it was late, and they still had dinner to make and homework to finish.

"Maybe another day, Emma," she said gently, feeling a twinge of reluctance herself. "We'll come back when we have more time."

Emma and Max groaned but nodded. Still, as they walked away, the family cast one last look over their shoulders at Tockman's Clocks. Inside, the shop's warm glow seemed to pulse gently, like a heartbeat.

And for just a moment, they thought they saw a shadowy figure in the window, watching them with a quiet, knowing smile.

As they turned the corner, the street fell silent, and the little shop returned to its usual stillness. But that evening, as the Baxters sat around their dinner table, the magic of the clock shop lingered in their minds, filling them with the thrilling anticipation of a mystery just waiting to unfold.

Chapter 2: The Mysterious Invitation

The following morning began like any other. The Baxter family hustled and bustled through their routines—Mr. Baxter gathered his papers and a travel mug of coffee, Mrs. Baxter packed lunches, Max hunted for his missing math homework, and Emma daydreamed while munching on a piece of toast. Despite the usual morning rush, the children couldn't stop thinking about Tockman's Clocks.

As they finally made their way down the familiar street, Emma looked eagerly at the shop, hoping for another glimpse of the mysterious clockmaker. To her disappointment, the shop looked as it always did in the morning—quiet and still, with the golden sign gently swinging in the breeze. Yet today, something seemed different, even though Emma couldn't quite put her finger on what.

As they neared the door, Max noticed a small, folded piece of paper lying on the sidewalk in front of the shop. "Hey, what's that?" he asked, bending down to pick it up.

The paper was delicate and yellowed at the edges, like it had been there for years, though it was perfectly clean. Scrawled in elegant, looping handwriting on the front were the words To the Baxter Family.

Max's eyes widened. "It's got our name on it!"

Mrs. Baxter frowned, glancing around as if expecting someone to appear. "How odd," she murmured, a little unsure of whether they should read the note or leave it be. But Emma, curiosity brimming, was already tugging at the edges, eager to see what was inside.

"Open it, open it!" she whispered excitedly, practically bouncing on her toes.

Max carefully unfolded the note. Inside, the handwriting was neat and old-fashioned, as if written by someone who had spent years perfecting each letter. It read:

Dear Baxter Family,

I have watched you pass by my little shop each day, and it warms my heart to see your curiosity about my clocks. I believe that each of you has a special relationship with time—one that I can help you explore.

If you are interested, I would be honoured to welcome you into Tockman's Clocks and share with you a most unique gift. I believe it is one that your family needs, even if you don't yet know it.

Please come when you are ready.

Warmly,

Mr. Tockman

The family fell silent as they read the note, each of them feeling a strange mixture of excitement and wonder. Emma held her breath, her eyes wide with delight. "A gift! He has a special gift for us! I knew he was magical."

Mrs. Baxter smiled at Emma's enthusiasm but couldn't help feeling intrigued herself. She didn't usually give much thought to clocks, but there was something about Mr. Tockman's note that drew her in. His words hinted at something more than just timepieces and gears. They felt... significant, as though he understood something about them that even they didn't know.

"Why would he give us a gift, though?" Max asked, frowning in thought. "I mean, we've never even been inside his shop."

Mr. Baxter adjusted his glasses, studying the note thoughtfully. "Maybe he's just friendly, and he's noticed that we've taken an interest in his shop," he suggested, though even he sounded a bit unsure. There was a mystery in Mr. Tockman's words that made him curious, too. A unique gift that their family needed? It was unlike anything he'd ever heard before.

"Well, I think we should go!" Emma declared, grinning from ear to ear. "What if he really does have something special, like a clock that can make time slow down?"

Mrs. Baxter laughed, tucking the note into her bag. "Maybe we will, Emma. But let's not rush. If he says to come when we're ready, we can take our time."

Emma pouted, but she understood. The idea of a special gift waiting for them in that mysterious little shop filled her with anticipation. For now, though, the family continued on their way, each of them sneaking glances back at Tockman's Clocks, feeling like something extraordinary was waiting just behind its door.

That evening, after the rush of homework and dinner had settled, the family found themselves sitting together in the cozy warmth of the living room. The note from Mr. Tockman rested on the coffee table, and every now and then, one of them would glance at it, their thoughts drifting to the little shop and its peculiar invitation.

"So, what do you guys think about Mr. Tockman's gift?" Mr. Baxter finally asked, breaking the silence.

Emma sat up, her eyes bright. "I think it's something magical. Maybe it's a clock that can stop time, or one that lets you travel back to a memory."

Max, always the practical one, rolled his eyes but couldn't hide a slight smile. "It's probably just a regular clock that he thinks we'll like."

Mrs. Baxter, who had been listening quietly, spoke up. "What if it's something different? I mean, he did say it was something our family needs, not just something we'd like. Maybe it's a way to help us spend more time together."

The family fell silent again, pondering her words. As much as they loved each other, life was busy. Mornings were rushed, and evenings were often filled with the demands of work and school. What if, somehow, Mr. Tockman's gift really could give them the time they were missing?

"Well, there's only one way to find out," Mr. Baxter said, giving a small smile. "Maybe this weekend, we can stop by and see what Mr. Tockman has in mind."

Emma clapped her hands, her excitement bubbling over. "Yes, yes, yes! I can't wait to meet him. I wonder if he really is a wizard."

Max smirked, nudging his sister. "Wizards aren't real, Emma."

Emma stuck her tongue out at him. "Maybe not, but he might be special."

They all laughed, but in the back of their minds, each family member felt a quiet thrill. There was something undeniably magical about the note and its invitation. It felt like a door had been opened, leading them toward something unknown and wonderful.

That night, as they each went to bed, they found themselves thinking about Tockman's Clocks. Emma lay awake, imagining all the enchanted clocks that might be hidden inside the shop, each one with its own magic. Max wondered about the clockmaker himself, curious if Mr. Tockman really did know some secrets about time. Mr. Baxter considered the odd wording of the note, wondering what Mr. Tockman thought their family needed. And Mrs. Baxter felt a warm sense of hope, as though the promise of something beautiful was just within reach.

For the next few days, they continued their usual routine, but they couldn't help glancing at Tockman's Clocks each time they passed. The shop seemed to hum with a quiet energy, its golden sign catching the light in a way that made it shimmer, almost like it was beckoning them.

Finally, on Saturday morning, the family gathered by the front door, each of them dressed warmly for the brisk autumn air. Mr. Baxter held the note from Mr. Tockman, rereading it one last time.

"Are we ready?" he asked, looking around at each of them.

Emma practically jumped up and down. "Yes! Let's go!"

Max nodded, trying to act calm but clearly just as eager.

Mrs. Baxter gave them all a warm smile. "Then let's go see what Mr. Tockman's gift is."

And so, with hearts full of excitement and a tinge of mystery, the Baxter family set off down the street. They walked side by side, feeling as though they were on the brink of something special. As they approached the shop, a soft breeze seemed to whisper through the air, and the faintest sound of ticking drifted toward them, like music from another world.

As they reached the front door of Tockman's Clocks, they paused, looking at each other one last time, knowing that whatever lay behind this door was going to be an adventure they would never forget.

But little did they know, Mr. Tockman's gift would change everything.

Chapter 3: Meeting the Clockmaker

The Baxter family stood in front of Tockman's Clocks, each of them feeling a mixture of excitement and wonder. The shop's door was slightly ajar, and the warm glow from within seemed to spill out onto the cobblestones, inviting them inside.

Mr. Baxter glanced at his family, gave a little nod, and pushed open the door. A soft chime sounded, like a small bell high above them, as they stepped into the shop. Instantly, they were surrounded by the gentle hum of ticking clocks. Some were slow and rhythmic, others were quick and lively, but together they created a soft, soothing melody that seemed to quiet the world around them.

The shop was unlike anything they had imagined. Clocks covered nearly every inch of the walls—grandfather clocks with polished wood cases, delicate pocket watches gleaming under glass, wall clocks with painted scenes of forests and mountains. The shelves were lined with small brass gears, tiny tools, and clock faces in various stages of repair. Every corner of the shop seemed to hold something fascinating, and the Baxters couldn't help but wander around, enchanted by the sight.

Emma's eyes sparkled as she took it all in. "It's like a dream," she whispered, reaching out to touch the glass case holding a collection of tiny silver watches.

Just then, a quiet voice spoke from behind them. "Welcome, Baxters. I've been waiting for you."

They turned to see an elderly man standing near the back of the shop, with kind eyes that seemed to twinkle behind round glasses. He wore a neatly pressed vest with brass buttons and had a bushy mustache that gave him a warm, friendly look. In one hand, he held a pocket watch, and in the other, a small tool that glinted in the light.

"Mr. Tockman?" Mrs. Baxter asked, her voice full of curiosity.

The old man nodded, his smile widening. "Yes, indeed. And you must be Emma, Max, Mr. Baxter, and Mrs. Baxter." He nodded to each of them, as if greeting old friends.

Max's eyes widened. "How do you know our names?"

Mr. Tockman chuckled, slipping the pocket watch into his vest pocket. "Ah, I've seen you passing by my shop every day. And besides, a clockmaker must always be good with names. Each name has its own rhythm, its own unique tick and tock, wouldn't you agree?"

Emma grinned, feeling as though she had just met someone out of one of her favorite storybooks. "Are you really a clockmaker? And do you really have a gift for us?"

Mr. Tockman's eyes twinkled. "Oh, I am indeed a clockmaker. A rather old one, I might add. And yes, I believe I do have something special just for you. But perhaps, before we talk about gifts, you'd like to see something unusual?"

The family nodded, curiosity practically spilling over. Mr. Tockman turned and led them through the shop, weaving around displays of clocks and tiny shelves filled with gears and springs, until they reached the very back of the shop. There, sitting on a low wooden table, was an old clock that looked unlike any other in the store.

The clock was large and round, with an intricately carved wooden frame. But it was worn and faded, with small cracks running across its face. Its hands, which seemed to be made of tarnished silver, were frozen in place, pointing to a time that didn't seem to make sense. It was as if the clock had been stopped for years, caught in a moment it couldn't escape.

Emma stared at the clock, her eyes wide. "It's... beautiful," she murmured, though she wasn't sure why she felt that way about such an old, broken thing.

Mr. Tockman smiled, resting his hand gently on the clock. "This clock has seen many years, and it has kept time for many people. But it stopped ticking long ago. Now, it's waiting—waiting for someone to see its value beyond its broken face."

Max frowned, leaning in closer to study the clock. "Why don't you just fix it?"

Mr. Tockman chuckled softly. "Ah, some clocks can be fixed with a few turns of a gear or a little oil. But others... they need something more. This one, in particular, requires a special touch. I've tried many times to get it ticking again, but I believe it's waiting for someone else to help it come to life."

Emma's heart fluttered as she gazed at the clock. "Someone else? Who?"

The clockmaker looked at each of them with a mysterious smile. "Perhaps someone who needs time, or perhaps a family who understands its importance. This clock holds a special gift within, you see, but it's only revealed to those who truly need it."

The Baxters exchanged curious glances, each of them feeling strangely drawn to the clock, as though it held a secret meant just for them. Mrs. Baxter noticed the unusual feeling growing in her chest, like a warm, hopeful tug. She'd often wished for a little more time in her day, especially with how busy life could be. Maybe, somehow, this clock really did hold the answer to that unspoken wish.

Max reached out, almost instinctively, and brushed his fingers along the edge of the clock. It was cool to the touch, and for a brief moment, he thought he felt the faintest vibration, like the hum of a heartbeat. He pulled his hand back, startled, but Mr. Tockman just smiled.

"It's an unusual feeling, isn't it?" the clockmaker said softly. "This clock has a way of connecting with people, of making them feel things they can't quite explain."

Mr. Baxter, who had been quietly observing, finally spoke. "Mr. Tockman, you mentioned a gift in the note. Is this... this clock, somehow, part of it?"

Mr. Tockman gave a slow nod. "In a way, yes. But gifts must be given with purpose. And before I can offer this clock to you, I must be certain that it's something your family truly needs."

"What do you mean by 'needs'?" Mrs. Baxter asked, her brow furrowing.

The clockmaker's expression softened. "Time is a curious thing, you see. We all have it, yet most of us feel as though we don't have enough. Some wish to go back, others want to move forward, and many just want to slow down. This clock... well, it's special because it offers a bit of flexibility with time. But only for those who genuinely need it."

Emma and Max exchanged excited looks, each of them wondering what "flexibility with time" could mean. The idea that the clock might be magical, that it could bend the rules of time itself, filled them with wonder.

"So... if we needed extra time—" Emma began, but Mr. Tockman held up a hand, a twinkle in his eye.

"Ah, but that's where the mystery lies. It isn't about wanting extra time; it's about knowing why you need it. The clock chooses who it will work for, and it only does so for those who understand its value."

The Baxters fell silent, each of them lost in their own thoughts. Mr. Tockman's words seemed to settle over them like a quiet, unspoken promise. They didn't fully understand what he meant, but they could sense that he was speaking from a place of deep wisdom.

Finally, Mr. Tockman took a step back, his gaze lingering on the clock. "Why don't you go home and think about it? The clock will still be here, waiting. When you're ready, you'll know if it's truly meant for you."

Emma felt a pang of disappointment, wanting to take the clock home with them right then and there. But as she looked up at Mr. Tockman's kind, knowing eyes, she felt a strange sense of peace. This was a journey they weren't meant to rush.

"Thank you, Mr. Tockman," Mr. Baxter said, shaking the clockmaker's hand. "We'll think about it."

The family left the shop, stepping back into the bustling street, but the world somehow felt a little different. The sound of the clocks ticking inside Tockman's Clocks seemed to follow them, lingering in the air like an echo.

And as they walked home, each of them felt that something extraordinary was waiting for them, just around the corner.

Chapter 4: The Gift of Time

The next morning, the Baxter family couldn't stop talking about Tockman's Clocks and the strange, enchanting clock that Mr. Tockman had shown them. The memory of the shop lingered in each of their minds, and more than once, they found themselves wondering what Mr. Tockman had meant about "those who understand the value of time."

By the end of the day, they decided to go back to the clock shop to see if Mr. Tockman would tell them more about the unusual clock and, perhaps, allow them to take it home. There was something about it that had left each of them feeling as though it was meant for them. They felt drawn back to the shop, as though the clock itself was waiting for their return.

As they entered Tockman's Clocks, the familiar melody of ticking sounds washed over them, filling the shop with a gentle, almost soothing rhythm. Mr. Tockman was standing at the counter, polishing a small silver watch. When he saw them, he gave a warm smile, as if he'd expected their return all along.

"Ah, the Baxter family," he greeted, his eyes twinkling behind his round glasses. "I wondered when I might see you again."

Emma stepped forward, her face full of excitement. "Mr. Tockman, we couldn't stop thinking about that clock you showed us. The broken one in the back. Can you tell us more about it?"

Mr. Tockman chuckled, setting down the silver watch. "Of course, my dear." He gestured for them to follow him to the back of the shop, where the old, broken clock sat on the same wooden table as before, its hands still frozen in place.

"This clock," he began, running his hand gently over the clock's wooden frame, "is quite unlike any other in my shop. It has a unique ability, one that allows it to bend time. But it only works for those who truly understand why they need it."

Mr. Baxter raised an eyebrow. "When you say it bends time... do you mean it actually slows down or speeds up time?"

Mr. Tockman nodded, his expression serious yet warm. "In a way, yes. For those who carry it, this clock can give them a bit of extra time when they need it most. It's not for frivolous uses, mind you, but for moments that truly matter. You see, the clock senses the intent of its keepers and will work only when it feels their need is genuine."

The family exchanged glances, each of them trying to imagine what that might mean for them. Max looked at the clock with wide eyes, trying to picture how it would feel to make time slow down, even just a little.

"So... you're saying this clock can slow down time if we're in a hurry?" he asked, his voice filled with wonder.

Mr. Tockman chuckled, a glint of amusement in his eyes. "Not exactly. It won't solve every hurried morning or help you finish every forgotten homework assignment. But in moments when you feel time slipping through your fingers—when you wish you could pause and truly be in the moment—this clock can help you do just that."

Mrs. Baxter's expression softened, and she gazed at the clock with newfound appreciation. As a busy parent juggling work and family, she'd often wished for a little more time to simply be with her loved ones, without the rush of daily responsibilities. The idea of having a tool that could offer her that gift, even for a few precious moments, made her heart ache with hope.

"So, what would we need to do?" Mr. Baxter asked, still looking at the clock with cautious curiosity.

Mr. Tockman smiled and lifted the clock gently, turning it toward the family. "It's simple. You just keep it close to you, somewhere in your home. When the moment comes, you'll know. The clock will help you recognize when it's time to slow down, to focus on what matters most. But remember, it's not a toy or something to be used without thought.

Its magic lies in helping you see the value of the time you have, not in giving you more of it."

He carefully held the clock out to them, his eyes warm and full of kindness. "I would like your family to have this clock as a gift. I believe it has chosen you, and I trust that you will honour its power with the respect it deserves."

Emma's eyes shone with excitement, and Max's jaw dropped as he reached out, gingerly touching the edge of the clock. Even Mr. and Mrs. Baxter seemed unable to hide their wonder and gratitude as they took in the significance of Mr. Tockman's offer.

"Thank you, Mr. Tockman," Mrs. Baxter said softly, her voice filled with emotion. "This... this is a beautiful gift. We'll take good care of it."

Mr. Tockman nodded, his expression both wise and gentle. "I know you will. Remember, it's the moments we create, not the minutes we count, that truly make up a life. This clock will remind you of that."

With the clock cradled carefully in Mrs. Baxter's arms, the family began to make their way toward the door. Just as they reached it, Emma turned back to Mr. Tockman, a question bubbling up inside her.

"Mr. Tockman, why did you choose us?" she asked, her voice quiet and curious.

The clockmaker looked at her, his gaze soft. "Because I saw something in your family that not everyone sees in themselves. You understand, even if only in a small way, that time is precious. I believe this clock will help you discover just how magical time can be when you share it with those you love."

Emma's heart swelled with gratitude, and she nodded, giving Mr. Tockman a smile that he returned with a wink. Then, with a gentle nudge, he closed the shop door behind them, watching as the Baxter family walked down the street with the clock in their arms, unaware of the adventure that lay ahead.

As they strolled home, each member of the family felt a quiet thrill of anticipation. They still didn't fully understand what the clock could do, but they knew it was something special, something they would have to learn as they went.

At home, they placed the clock on a shelf in the living room, where it seemed to belong instantly, as though it had always been a part of their family. Emma and Max sat cross-legged on the floor, staring at it in awe, as if waiting for it to spring to life. Mr. and Mrs. Baxter shared a quiet glance, feeling a deep, unspoken hope that this clock would bring them closer together in ways they couldn't yet imagine.

And that night, as they went about their usual routines, a warm feeling of peace settled over their home. It was as though the presence of the clock had softened the edges of time, allowing them to relax and simply enjoy being together.

They didn't yet know how the clock would change their lives, or what moments it would help them capture. But for the first time in a long time, the Baxters felt as though time was on their side.

And somewhere, back in his little shop, Mr. Tockman sat by the light of his own ticking clocks, a smile playing on his lips as he thought of the family and the gift of time that was now theirs.

Chapter 5: Rules of the Clock

The Baxter family sat together in the cozy warmth of their living room, the newly gifted clock placed carefully on the shelf where everyone could see it. The old, broken clock was unlike anything they had ever owned. Its face was cracked, its hands frozen at a peculiar time, and yet, there was a strange beauty in its age and imperfections. It seemed to radiate a quiet strength, as though it held secrets just waiting to be uncovered.

Emma leaned in, staring at the clock with wide eyes. "Do you think it will start working on its own?" she asked, her voice filled with awe.

Max shook his head, watching it just as intently. "Mr. Tockman said it only works when we 'truly need more time.' What does that even mean?"

Mrs. Baxter gave a thoughtful nod, glancing from the clock to her children. "It's a good question, Max. I think Mr. Tockman was trying to remind us that we shouldn't use it just because we're in a hurry or because we feel rushed. He meant for us to be mindful."

Mr. Baxter crossed his arms, thinking back to the clockmaker's words. "He seemed very serious about it. 'Truly need more time'... I suppose it means we can't use it for small things. It's for when time feels especially important—maybe moments we don't want to rush."

Emma's face lit up as she thought it over. "Like... like maybe a birthday, or a special family day?"

Mrs. Baxter smiled, nodding. "Yes, exactly. It might be meant for those days when we're all together, making memories that we don't want to let slip by too quickly."

Max frowned, still a bit puzzled. "But what if I have a test at school and I need more time to finish it? Or what if I'm late to class?"

Mr. Baxter chuckled. "I don't think Mr. Tockman intended for it to be a homework helper, Max. This isn't a clock for everyday things or things we should be responsible for ourselves."

Max nodded slowly, beginning to understand. "So... it's for really important times. Things that matter to all of us. Not just stuff that would make my life easier."

Emma's eyes sparkled as she thought about the possibilities. "So if we can only use it when we really need more time, that means it can't be for silly reasons or just because we want to. Mr. Tockman said it has to be about something that matters. Something we'd remember."

The family fell silent, each of them letting the idea settle over them. The clock was indeed a gift, but it came with a weighty responsibility. They would have to be careful, thoughtful, and perhaps even a little wise about how they used it. The thought of being given extra time—a magical extension of a precious moment—felt like something rare and valuable, something not to be taken lightly.

After a few moments, Mr. Baxter leaned forward, his voice soft but firm. "I think we need some rules, then, to help us remember Mr. Tockman's words. If this clock really can slow down time, we should use it only when we're all agreed on it."

The children nodded eagerly, each of them feeling the importance of this gift in their own way. Mrs. Baxter reached out to hold Emma and Max's hands, a warm, motherly smile on her face. "Agreed. It should be something special that we all decide on together. If we feel rushed on any ordinary day, we should try to slow down ourselves first, without using the clock."

Max grinned, excited by the challenge. "Yeah, we can try to make more time for each other even without magic. That way, if we really do need it someday, the clock will be ready."

Emma clapped her hands together. "So, if we all agree, then the clock will... just work?"

The family exchanged glances, none of them entirely sure how the clock's magic worked. Mr. Tockman had been vague, and perhaps that was part of the mystery. But somehow, they each felt that when the time came, they would know. The clock would be ready for them, waiting to make a special moment last a little longer.

"Maybe we should make a list of the kinds of times we think would be important enough," Max suggested thoughtfully.

They began to brainstorm, sharing moments that might feel worthy of using the clock's magic. Birthdays, family holidays, or quiet nights spent reading stories together. They talked about special trips or celebrations, and even the simple moments when they were all together, laughing or enjoying each other's company. They each shared their ideas, coming to understand just how much these shared moments meant to them.

After a while, Emma's eyes grew wide with excitement. "What if one day we're all having such a wonderful time, and we feel like it's going too fast? Then we'll know that's when we really need it!"

Mrs. Baxter nodded, her heart warm with love for her family. "Yes, Emma. When we feel like the time is just too precious to let go of, that's when we'll know."

The family sat in thoughtful silence for a moment, letting the importance of their decision settle in. The clock rested on the shelf, quietly watching, as if it already understood the love and care the Baxters would pour into their special moments. It didn't tick, nor did its hands move, but somehow, it felt alive, patiently waiting for the day it would be called into service.

Finally, Mr. Baxter cleared his throat, smiling around at his family. "So it's decided, then. The clock is for when we're all together and we feel we truly need to slow down and enjoy the moment. We'll make that decision as a family, and we'll honour it."

Emma and Max nodded eagerly, a solemn sense of excitement filling the room. They were more than ready to take on the responsibility, and they felt a thrill at the idea that someday, when the time was right, they would use the clock to experience a magical moment that would last just a little bit longer.

That night, as they all prepared for bed, the family felt a closeness they hadn't felt in a while. Even as they said their goodnights and climbed under the covers, they each found their thoughts drifting back to the clock on the shelf, sitting quietly in the dim light of the living room.

The clock hadn't moved, and yet it seemed to radiate a gentle warmth, like a quiet promise that it would be there whenever they needed it most. Its magic wasn't about granting endless wishes or letting them escape from the ordinary moments in life. Instead, it offered something much rarer: the chance to slow down, to be fully present, and to savour the time they shared as a family.

As they drifted off to sleep, each of them dreamed of the special moments they would share, the laughter, the stories, the quiet warmth of togetherness. And in the soft shadows of the living room, the clock waited, patient and still, its secret magic quietly humming in the background.

When the time came, it would be ready. For now, it was content to sit and watch over the Baxter family, like a guardian of the moments that truly mattered.

Part 2: Discovering the Magic
Chapter 6: A Hectic Morning

The Baxter household was rarely quiet in the morning. From the moment the first alarm buzzed, it was a flurry of activity. Today, however, was shaping up to be especially chaotic.

Mr. Baxter groaned as his alarm went off, his hand fumbling for the snooze button before he finally gave in to the inevitable. Across the hall, Mrs. Baxter was already awake, tugging on her work clothes while juggling her phone, which was pinging with early morning emails.

"Emma, Max, time to get up!" she called, balancing a hairbrush in one hand and her phone in the other.

In the kids' room, Emma slowly sat up, her curls tousled from sleep. Max, still wrapped in his blanket like a cocoon, groaned and pulled his pillow over his head. "Five more minutes," he mumbled, hoping for just a little more sleep.

But there was no time to spare. In the kitchen, cereal bowls clinked, the toaster popped, and the smell of brewing coffee filled the air. Emma stumbled in, bleary-eyed, holding her favorite storybook, and absentmindedly poured orange juice over her cereal instead of milk. Max shuffled in behind her, still yawning as he tried to smooth down his messy hair with one hand.

Mrs. Baxter glanced at her watch, her voice growing tense. "Emma, eat your breakfast. Max, brush your hair, and please don't forget your math homework this time!" she urged.

Emma started to reply, but Mr. Baxter rushed in, looking half-awake and clutching his coffee like a lifeline. "Where are my keys? And has anyone seen my briefcase?" he asked, his gaze darting around the kitchen as he frantically looked under papers and around the counter.

In the midst of the clamour, the old clock on the shelf sat quietly, its cracked face and still hands seeming to watch over the family. None of the Baxters noticed the faint glow that began to emanate from it, as though the clock sensed the rising tension and had decided it was time to intervene.

Just as Mr. Baxter bumped into Max, nearly spilling his coffee, something strange happened. The air around them seemed to shift, softening, as if an invisible hand had pressed "pause" on the rush of the morning. The hum of the refrigerator grew quiet, the ticking of the kitchen clock slowed, and even the sunlight streaming through the window seemed to settle into a softer, gentler glow.

At first, they didn't realize what was happening. Mrs. Baxter was pouring another cup of coffee, but as she brought the cup to her lips, she noticed a feeling of calm washing over her, as though a weight had lifted from her shoulders. She took a deep breath, realizing, almost in disbelief, that she felt… unhurried.

"Wait," she murmured, glancing at her watch. The hands seemed to have slowed, as if time itself had taken a deep breath and relaxed.

Emma, who had been stirring her orange juice and cereal with a sigh, looked up. "Mom, it feels like… like there's more time. Doesn't it?"

Max, finally wide awake, looked around, a puzzled expression on his face. "It's like everything just… slowed down," he said, feeling the strange, warm calm settle over him. Even his stomach stopped its anxious churning about his math test.

Mr. Baxter blinked, looking around the kitchen. He realized he was still holding his coffee cup, but suddenly, there was no need to rush. Instead, he placed his cup down and took a seat at the table. "Why don't we all sit down?" he suggested, surprising even himself with his relaxed tone.

The children exchanged glances, half-expecting their parents to snap back into their usual rushed routines. But the urgency had vanished, replaced by a quiet, almost magical sense of peace. They joined their father at the table, settling into their seats.

Mrs. Baxter poured herself another cup of coffee, feeling calmer than she had in ages. "Maybe we can just... take a few minutes together," she said softly. "I don't think the world will end if we're a little slower today."

Emma grinned, delighted. "I'd love that! We never have time to just talk in the morning."

As they sat around the table, breakfast took on a different feel. They laughed about Emma's orange-juice cereal mishap, and Max told them about his math test, feeling proud of the studying he'd done. Mr. Baxter shared a funny story from work that made everyone laugh, and Mrs. Baxter found herself smiling in a way she hadn't in a long time.

They hadn't felt this connected, this together, in ages. And none of them noticed the quiet glow that still radiated from the old clock on the shelf, its broken hands unmoving yet somehow more alive than ever.

After a while, Mrs. Baxter glanced at the clock on the wall. "Well, I suppose we should start getting ready," she said, surprised to find that there was still plenty of time left. She stood up, refreshed, and watched as her family, now moving with a gentle, unhurried pace, went about gathering their things for the day.

Emma walked over to the old clock on the shelf, gently touching its cracked face. "Do you think it was... helping us just now?" she asked quietly, looking at Max.

Max nodded, feeling a strange certainty settle over him. "I think so. I don't know how, but it feels like it gave us extra time, just for this morning."

Mr. Baxter joined them, giving the clock a thoughtful look. "Maybe Mr. Tockman's gift was just showing us how nice it can be to slow down," he said, smiling at his family. "I think it reminded us that we don't always need to rush."

Mrs. Baxter placed a gentle hand on the clock, feeling grateful for this unexpected moment. "If we really need more time, it seems like the clock is ready to help. But maybe we can try to create more moments like this on our own."

Emma nodded, her face bright with a new idea. "Maybe if we just try to slow down, we won't need magic every time. We can make a rule to have breakfast together whenever we can!"

Max grinned, his eyes lighting up. "Yeah! And then, if we really need it—like if we're having the best day ever and don't want it to end—then maybe the clock will work for us again."

The family gathered their bags and stepped out the door, but today, the walk felt different. There was no rush, no hurry to get where they needed to go. They walked together, chatting, laughing, and enjoying the cool morning air, as if time were expanding around them like a warm bubble.

As they rounded the corner, they couldn't help but glance back at their home, where the old clock sat patiently on the shelf, quiet and still. Somehow, they all knew it was watching over them, a reminder of the gift they'd been given: the gift of time, both magical and ordinary, to savour whenever they needed it most.

And with this newfound perspective, they continued on their way, each of them carrying the magic of that quiet morning in their hearts, ready to cherish more of the moments that made life precious.

Chapter 7: Mom's Special Day

It was a rainy Wednesday afternoon, and Mrs. Baxter sat at the dining room table, surrounded by papers, a laptop, and half-finished notes scrawled on sticky pads. Her face was tense as she tapped her fingers, staring at her laptop screen with growing anxiety. She had a big project due the next morning, one she'd been working on for weeks, but as the deadline loomed closer, she felt less and less prepared.

Mr. Baxter watched her from the kitchen, concern etched on his face. It wasn't often that his wife seemed this overwhelmed. She was usually calm, handling her work responsibilities with grace, but tonight, the stress was weighing heavily on her.

"Are you alright?" he asked gently, walking over to her.

Mrs. Baxter sighed, rubbing her temples. "I'm just... I don't know if I can finish this tonight. There's so much left to do, and I've barely made any progress. I've been putting this off, thinking I'd have time, and now... well, I don't."

Emma and Max peeked around the corner, picking up on the tension. They glanced at each other, sharing a worried look. Their mother was always there to help them, whether it was with homework, school projects, or anything else they needed. Seeing her so stressed and frustrated was unusual, and it made them feel like they should do something to help.

Emma tiptoed into the room, giving her mom a warm hug. "Maybe you just need a little extra time, Mom," she said softly.

Mrs. Baxter smiled, ruffling Emma's hair. "Oh, if only I could have a few more hours tonight. But there's no way to make that happen, is there?"

At her words, Mr. Baxter's gaze drifted over to the shelf in the living room, where the old clock sat quietly, as if waiting. Its cracked face and unmoving hands were still as ever, but he couldn't shake the feeling that perhaps it could help, just as it had on that hectic morning not too long ago.

"Maybe..." he murmured, glancing at Emma and Max, "maybe the clock could help again."

Mrs. Baxter looked up, surprised. "You mean... Mr. Tockman's clock?"

Mr. Baxter nodded, a small smile tugging at his lips. "The last time we really needed it, it seemed to know. Maybe it would give you that extra time you need tonight. Just enough to help you finish the project without feeling so rushed."

Mrs. Baxter looked sceptical, but her heart softened as she glanced at the old clock on the shelf. She had felt its magic once already, and the memory of that peaceful morning filled her with hope. If it truly had the power to bend time, maybe it would grant her just a few extra hours—enough to complete her project and put her worries to rest.

She nodded slowly. "It's worth a try, I suppose. I'll do my best to stay focused, and maybe... maybe the clock will help if I really need it."

With a deep breath, she returned to her laptop, diving back into her work. The rest of the family retreated to give her some quiet, but they couldn't resist sneaking peeks from the doorway, curious to see if the clock would work its magic once more.

As Mrs. Baxter typed, the rain pattered softly against the windows, and the house grew still. She focused completely on her project, blocking out everything else as she pored over the documents in front of her. The more she worked, the calmer she felt, as if an invisible hand were guiding her, helping her see solutions she hadn't noticed before.

Suddenly, a gentle warmth filled the room, and the familiar ticking sound echoed from the living room shelf. The old clock began to emit a soft glow, its cracked face glimmering faintly. Mrs. Baxter looked up, catching the clock's gentle light in the corner of her eye. The hands hadn't moved, but somehow, time itself seemed to stretch, slowing down as if to accommodate her needs.

Her racing thoughts quieted, and the weight of the deadline lifted, replaced by a steady sense of calm. With each passing minute, she felt more focused, her mind clear and her ideas flowing freely. She glanced at her watch, noticing that the minutes seemed to be moving slower than usual. She took a deep breath, feeling the tension in her shoulders melt away as she typed at a comfortable pace, the pressure easing as the magic of the clock surrounded her.

Emma and Max peeked into the room, their eyes widening at the soft glow that emanated from the clock. They exchanged excited looks, thrilled to see the magic unfolding before their eyes.

"Look, it's working!" Max whispered, nudging Emma.

Emma beamed, watching her mother work with a newfound sense of peace. "It's like the clock is giving her extra time, just like she needed."

Mr. Baxter joined them, his heart swelling with gratitude. Seeing his wife's tension fade and her confidence grow was a gift in itself. He could see the effect the clock was having on her, slowing down the rush of time and creating a quiet, focused space for her to complete her work.

For the next few hours, Mrs. Baxter worked steadily, unaware of the unusual flow of time around her. She lost herself in her project, pouring her energy and focus into each line she wrote. When she finally finished the last piece of the project, she leaned back with a deep sigh of relief, feeling a sense of accomplishment and calm.

The clock's glow faded, and the ticking softened, returning the room to its ordinary stillness. The hands remained frozen, but everyone could feel that its work had been done.

Mrs. Baxter glanced at the time, astonished to see that she had finished well before midnight. "I... I can't believe it," she murmured, glancing at the clock with gratitude. "I thought I'd be working all night. It felt like I had hours and hours to work, and I didn't even feel rushed."

Emma and Max rushed to her side, hugging her tightly. "The clock helped you, Mom! It really gave you extra time, just like we thought it would!" Emma said, her eyes shining with excitement.

Mr. Baxter placed a hand on his wife's shoulder, smiling warmly. "Looks like the clock knew exactly when to step in. I think it sensed how important this project was to you and granted you the time you needed to finish it without stress."

Mrs. Baxter gazed at the old clock on the shelf, feeling a deep gratitude for its quiet magic. She realized, in that moment, that the clock was more than just a gift; it was a reminder of what truly mattered. Time wasn't just about moving from one task to the next—it was about finding calm and focus, about honouring the moments that deserved to be cherished.

She turned to her family, pulling them into a warm embrace. "Thank you, all of you. I couldn't have done it without your encouragement—and without our magical little friend here," she added, nodding toward the clock.

As they all gathered around the clock, a gentle silence filled the room, like a soft reminder of the clock's magic and the gratitude it had inspired. The family held hands, feeling the warmth of each other's presence and the comfort of knowing that they could count on each other, and the clock, whenever they truly needed it.

That night, Mrs. Baxter went to bed with a light heart, feeling grateful for her family and the quiet magic that had given her peace when she needed it most. And as the house settled into silence, the clock watched over them, its timeless presence a gentle reminder that sometimes, all they needed was a little more time to truly live and savour the moments that mattered.

The Baxter family drifted off to sleep, each of them feeling a little closer, a little more grateful for the gift of time that connected them in the most meaningful ways. And the old clock, patient and still, waited quietly, ready to help whenever it was needed again.

Chapter 8: A Day of Play

Saturday morning dawned bright and sunny, with golden light streaming through the windows. Emma and Max were already awake, sitting at the breakfast table, filled with excitement about the day ahead. It was the first free weekend they'd had in a while, and they were both eager to spend it outside, playing and exploring.

"What should we do first?" Max asked, practically bouncing in his seat. "We could play hide-and-seek, or go to the park, or maybe build a fort!"

Emma grinned, equally thrilled. "Let's do all of it! We have the whole day to play. And maybe…" She glanced over at the shelf where the old clock sat, its cracked face gleaming faintly in the morning light. "Maybe we can use the clock to make today last a little longer."

Max's eyes lit up. "Do you think we could? I mean, we're not in a hurry or anything, but… it would be amazing if the day could last forever."

They glanced at their parents, who were finishing their coffee with knowing smiles.

"I think it's a perfect day for you two to try out the clock's magic," Mrs. Baxter said, her eyes warm. "But remember what Mr. Tockman said: the clock's magic only works when you're truly savouring the time you spend together."

Mr. Baxter added, "As long as you promise to enjoy each moment and not take it for granted, the clock might just grant you a little extra time today."

Emma and Max nodded eagerly, feeling a sense of excitement and responsibility. They both knew that this day was special, and they were determined to make the most of it.

They each gave their parents a quick hug, then darted off outside with the clock. The air was crisp and warm, and the neighbourhood was alive with the sounds of birds chirping and children playing in the distance. Holding the clock carefully, they made their way to their favorite spot under the big oak tree in the backyard. The tree had branches perfect for climbing, and it cast a beautiful, dappled shade over the grassy area below.

Emma held the clock gently in her lap, feeling its silent weight and watching it's still hands. "Okay, clock," she whispered, almost as if she were speaking to a friend. "We're ready to have a really special day. Could you help us make it last just a little bit longer?"

They sat quietly for a moment, waiting, as a gentle breeze stirred the leaves above. Then, almost imperceptibly, the air around them seemed to soften, as though the whole world had taken a deep breath and slowed down. The light streaming through the trees looked a little warmer, a little brighter, and the sounds around them seemed to grow quieter, blending into a peaceful hum.

Max grinned, feeling a strange, wonderful calm settling over them. "I think it worked," he said, his voice hushed. "It feels like time is stretching out, like we have all the time in the world."

Emma smiled, nodding. "Then let's make the most of it."

They started with hide-and-seek, darting between trees and bushes, taking their time to find the best hiding spots. Emma climbed up into the branches of the oak tree, giggling as she watched Max search for her below, calling her name as he peered under bushes and behind the garden shed.

When he finally spotted her, he burst into laughter. "I can't believe you climbed up there! You're going to have to show me how you did it."

For the next hour, they took turns climbing, helping each other find footholds and laughing as they pretended to be explorers in a magical forest. The clock's magic made them feel as though each moment were unfolding at its own perfect pace. There was no rush, no need to move on to the next activity; instead, they felt a quiet joy in simply being where they were.

After climbing, they built a fort out of blankets and cushions in the backyard. The fort became their castle, then a secret hideout, and finally, a cozy nook where they could lay side by side, looking up at the sky through a small gap in the blankets. Time seemed to melt away as they told stories, giggled, and talked about their favorite adventures.

"Do you think every day could feel like this?" Emma asked, her eyes dreamy as she gazed up at the soft blue sky.

Max shook his head thoughtfully. "I think it's special because we don't get days like this all the time. If we did, maybe it wouldn't feel this magical."

Emma nodded, feeling grateful for this day and the slow, peaceful magic of the clock. "You're right. I guess that's why Mr. Tockman wanted us to only use it when we really needed it."

They spent the rest of the afternoon at the park, playing on the swings and racing each other across the grass. Every laugh, every breath, every moment felt rich and full, as if each second had been stretched out to hold more joy than they'd ever imagined. By the time they finally returned home, the afternoon sun was just beginning to set, casting a golden glow over the house and yard.

Their parents were waiting for them on the porch, smiles lighting up their faces as Emma and Max ran up the steps, their cheeks flushed and eyes sparkling.

"How was your day?" Mrs. Baxter asked, hugging them both tightly.

Emma beamed, holding up the clock. "It was the best day ever. The clock made everything feel... longer. Like we had enough time to really enjoy everything."

Max nodded. "We didn't feel rushed, and we got to play and explore and do everything we wanted to. It was amazing."

Mr. Baxter gave them an approving nod. "That's the magic of unhurried time. Sometimes, when we slow down and just enjoy what's right in front of us, we realize we already have all the time we need."

Emma and Max glanced at each other, feeling the truth of their father's words. They had experienced an entire day without a single moment of hurry or worry. It was a gift they hadn't expected, and one they knew they'd treasure.

As they handed the clock back to their parents to place on the shelf, Emma gently touched its face, feeling a rush of gratitude. "Thank you," she whispered, knowing somehow that the clock understood her thanks.

That night, as they lay in bed, Emma and Max reflected on their magical day. They felt grateful for the simple moments, for the laughter they had shared, and for the chance to spend an entire day in each other's company without the usual rush of daily life. They realized that, while the clock had granted them extra time, it had also taught them a beautiful lesson: sometimes, the best way to enjoy life is to slow down and savour every second.

As they drifted off to sleep, they carried the warmth of their unhurried day with them, and the knowledge that they didn't always need magic to make a day special. Sometimes, all it took was a little bit of mindfulness, a lot of love, and the willingness to let each moment unfold at its own perfect pace.

Chapter 9: A Warning from Mr. Tockman

The Baxter family felt closer than ever after their magical day of play. The clock had given them the rare gift of unhurried time, allowing them to savour every moment of joy and laughter. But as grateful as they were, they couldn't shake the feeling that they owed Mr. Tockman a visit, both to thank him and to share the stories of their experience with the clock's magic.

That Saturday morning, they walked down the cobbled street toward Tockman's Clocks, each of them carrying memories of the wonderful moments they had shared. Emma and Max were particularly eager, with stories practically spilling over as they made their way to the little shop.

The golden sign above the shop door swung gently in the breeze, catching the morning light in its delicate script: Tockman's Clocks: Timepieces and Wonders. The door chimed softly as they stepped inside, greeted by the familiar tick-tock of countless clocks. They found Mr. Tockman behind the counter, carefully adjusting a small pocket watch with his usual calm focus.

When he looked up and saw them, a gentle smile spread across his face, and his eyes sparkled with recognition. "Ah, the Baxter family. I had a feeling I might see you today."

"Mr. Tockman!" Emma said, nearly bouncing with excitement. "We had the most amazing day! The clock—your clock—gave us extra time, and it felt like we got to play all day without any hurry!"

Max chimed in, his face full of excitement. "Yeah, it made everything feel longer and better. It was the best day we've had in... well, ever!"

Mr. Tockman listened to their stories, nodding slowly as they recounted each moment of their special day. His gaze softened, and a faint smile tugged at the corners of his mouth as he heard how the clock had allowed them to fully enjoy their time together.

"I'm very glad to hear that, my dears," he said, his voice warm. "It sounds like the clock did just what it was meant to do. When used thoughtfully, its magic can indeed help us see the beauty in each moment."

Mrs. Baxter smiled, feeling a deep gratitude for the gift Mr. Tockman had given their family. "Thank you, Mr. Tockman. We've all felt closer since we started using the clock. It's made us realize how precious time really is."

Mr. Tockman gave a small nod, but his expression turned a bit more serious as he set down the pocket watch he had been working on. He looked at the family, his eyes gentle yet full of wisdom. "I'm very pleased to hear that, Mrs. Baxter, but there is something important I must tell you all."

The family fell silent, sensing the shift in his tone.

Mr. Tockman folded his hands, looking from one family member to the next. "The clock is indeed a wonderful gift, but like all magical things, it has its limitations. Its power is meant to be a gentle nudge, a reminder to slow down and cherish what you have. But it is not something to be relied upon too often."

Max tilted his head, curious. "What do you mean?"

Mr. Tockman's gaze softened, and he spoke slowly, choosing his words with care. "Time is precious precisely because it is limited. If you rely on the clock too often, it may start to lose its magic, and you may find yourselves rushing again, even with the clock's help. It is only meant to enhance the moments that truly matter, not to replace the time you already have."

Emma bit her lip, her excitement fading as she took in Mr. Tockman's words. "So... we shouldn't use it all the time? Even if it makes things better?"

Mr. Tockman nodded gently. "Exactly, Emma. The magic of the clock lies in its ability to help you see the beauty in the time you already have. If you rely on it too often, you might lose that appreciation. And over time, its power could fade. Magic, you see, has a way of reminding us to be responsible. It wants us to grow and learn, not to depend on it."

Mrs. Baxter looked thoughtful, understanding the deeper meaning in Mr. Tockman's words. "So, we should use it sparingly, and only when we truly need it."

"Yes," he said, his expression calm but serious. "The clock is a gentle friend, not a solution to every problem. I want you to remember this: the most meaningful moments don't come from extending time, but from how you choose to live within the time you have. Let the clock be a guide, but not a crutch."

Mr. Baxter gave a nod of agreement, glancing at his children with a warm smile. "I think we can all do that. We'll keep the clock as a reminder to appreciate the time we have, but we'll try not to rely on it too much."

Emma and Max exchanged glances, both of them understanding the importance of what Mr. Tockman had said. Their day of play had been wonderful, but they realized that part of what made it special was the rare magic of the clock. If they used it too often, that magic might start to feel ordinary, and they didn't want to lose that sense of wonder.

Emma looked up at Mr. Tockman, nodding. "We promise to use it carefully."

Max chimed in, giving a resolute nod. "Yeah. Only when it really matters."

Mr. Tockman's face softened into a smile, and he reached out to place a gentle hand on each of their shoulders. "I'm proud of you both. You've already learned something very important. Now, remember this lesson, and keep the magic alive by using it wisely."

The family felt a sense of gratitude and understanding as Mr. Tockman's words settled over them. They realized that the true gift of the clock wasn't just in stretching moments—it was in teaching them to cherish each second they already had.

As they left the shop, the family walked together, holding onto the warmth of Mr. Tockman's words. They knew that the clock would still be there, waiting for those moments when they needed it most. But they also knew that, even without its magic, they had the power to slow down and appreciate the beauty of each day.

That evening, back at home, the clock sat quietly on the shelf, its face turned toward the family as if watching over them. They each took a moment to glance at it, feeling a new sense of respect and reverence for the quiet power it held.

And with Mr. Tockman's gentle reminder in their hearts, they resolved to make each moment count—not just the magical ones, but all the ordinary ones, too.

Chapter 10: The Clock Goes Wrong

The Baxter family had done their best to honour Mr. Tockman's advice, using the clock sparingly and only for truly special occasions. But one crisp fall afternoon, they felt it might be the right moment to turn to the clock's magic again.

It was a family day they had planned for weeks, with nothing but quality time on the agenda: board games, baking cookies, and a movie to cap off the evening. The day had started perfectly. They laughed together over breakfast, played Emma's favorite board game, and had even taken a short walk through the crunchy autumn leaves in their neighbourhood.

But as the afternoon slipped by, they realized that time was moving faster than they had anticipated. Mr. Baxter glanced at the clock on the wall, noticing with dismay that the day seemed to be slipping away. They hadn't even started the movie yet, and it was already early evening.

"Oh no, we're running out of time!" Emma said, her face falling as she looked out the window at the setting sun.

Max frowned, feeling the same pang of disappointment. "We didn't get to do everything. It feels like the day just flew by."

Mrs. Baxter shared a look with Mr. Baxter, sighing softly. "We wanted this day to last longer. Maybe..." She hesitated, glancing at the old clock on the shelf. "Maybe just this once, we could use the clock to slow down time."

Mr. Baxter nodded, his expression thoughtful. "I think we could. We've been careful, and this day really is important to us. What do you say, kids?"

Emma and Max both nodded eagerly. They had learned from Mr. Tockman's warning and felt that they understood the clock's magic better now. This wasn't just about wanting more time—it was about savouring a precious family day, something that didn't come around often.

Mrs. Baxter lifted the clock carefully from the shelf, holding it in her hands with reverence. They gathered around it, taking a moment to appreciate the beauty of the day they'd shared so far.

"Alright, clock," Mrs. Baxter whispered, a smile on her face. "Help us slow down, just for a little while longer."

The family waited, feeling the familiar warmth of the clock radiate from its face. But instead of the soft, calm sense of time slowing, a strange shiver ran through the room. The hands of the clock, usually frozen in place, began to tremble, and then, suddenly, they started spinning forward, faster and faster.

Emma's eyes widened. "Wait, it's... speeding up!"

The familiar comforting calm was replaced by a strange sense of urgency, as though they were being pulled forward, time slipping through their fingers faster than they could catch it. The daylight outside dimmed more rapidly than it should have, and shadows began to stretch across the walls.

"Oh no!" Max cried, looking around in confusion. "It's going the wrong way!"

The cozy, unhurried atmosphere they had hoped for turned into a frantic rush. They tried to keep playing their game, but it felt like time was pushing them ahead, faster than they could enjoy the moment. Mrs. Baxter quickly stood up, setting the clock back on the shelf with a worried expression.

"It's not working the way it usually does," she said, her face creased with concern. "Instead of slowing down, it's making everything speed up."

Mr. Baxter checked his watch, watching the minutes tick by at an unnaturally quick pace. "It's almost as if the clock's telling us we've used it too soon, or that this moment wasn't quite the right one for its magic."

Emma's face fell as she looked out the window, where the sky was already shifting to twilight. "But we just wanted more time together," she whispered, a pang of disappointment in her voice.

Mrs. Baxter placed a comforting arm around Emma's shoulders. "I know, sweetheart. I know. But maybe this is a reminder from the clock—maybe we weren't meant to use its magic for every special day."

Max looked at the clock with a mixture of disappointment and respect. "Maybe it's trying to tell us that we have to make the time we have special, instead of relying on magic to make it longer."

Mr. Baxter nodded, his face thoughtful. "It seems like the clock has a mind of its own. And today, it's teaching us that we can't always depend on it. Sometimes, we just have to let time move at its own pace."

The family sat in a quiet, reflective silence, realizing that even magic had its limits. They had taken Mr. Tockman's warning to heart, but perhaps they hadn't fully understood it until now. The clock's magic wasn't a tool to be used lightly, and today, it seemed to be reminding them of that lesson in a way they wouldn't forget.

As the last rays of sunlight faded, casting the room in a cozy glow, they decided to put the clock back on the shelf and finish their family day without it. They went on to bake cookies together, filling the house with the sweet, warm scent of vanilla and chocolate. They laughed over spilled flour, licked spoons, and played a few more rounds of their game, letting each moment be exactly as it was, without trying to change or extend it.

By the time they sat down to watch their movie, the earlier rush had faded, replaced by a deeper appreciation for the time they did have. They might not have been able to stretch out the day with magic, but they found that savouring each moment made it feel rich and full all on its own.

As they sat together on the couch, cozy under blankets with bowls of fresh cookies, Mrs. Baxter leaned over and kissed Emma and Max on their heads.

"Today taught us something important," she whispered. "We don't always need magic to make the most of our time. We just need to be present and make every moment count."

Emma snuggled closer, nodding with a sleepy smile. "I think I like it better this way. Magic is wonderful, but... I like just being here with all of you."

Max grinned, taking another bite of his cookie. "Yeah, me too. I guess the clock was just reminding us to make the most of the time we already have."

Mr. Baxter smiled, wrapping his arm around them. "Exactly. Sometimes, all we need is right in front of us."

The clock sat silently on the shelf, as if satisfied with the lesson it had delivered. Its hands remained still, the warm glow from the candles casting soft shadows over its face. The Baxter family finished their evening with grateful hearts, feeling closer than ever, having learned a valuable lesson from their magical friend.

As they drifted off to sleep that night, they carried with them a newfound respect for the flow of time. The clock had reminded them that while magic could make moments last, true magic lay in their ability to treasure those moments themselves.

And from its quiet place on the shelf, the clock watched over them, waiting patiently for the next time they would need its gentle reminder.

Part 3: Learning from Time
Chapter 11: Fixing the Clock

The following Saturday, the Baxter family made their way to Tockman's Clocks, carrying the old clock carefully in their arms. After the previous week's strange experience, they felt a mixture of respect, worry, and a desire to understand the clock's unexpected reaction. Although it had always been a little mysterious, they now realized that they didn't fully understand its powers—and they wondered if Mr. Tockman might help clarify why it had sped up time instead of slowing it down.

The shop's familiar golden sign swung gently in the morning breeze as they approached, its lettering glowing softly in the sunlight. Emma held the clock carefully as they entered, each of them silently hoping that Mr. Tockman would know exactly what had gone wrong.

The little bell over the door chimed as they stepped inside, and the cozy ticking of clocks surrounded them. Mr. Tockman looked up from his workbench, a warm smile spreading across his face as he saw them.

"Ah, the Baxter family! I was wondering when you might come by," he said, standing up and brushing his hands on his vest. "And I see you've brought the clock with you."

Emma nodded, her expression earnest. "We tried to use it again, Mr. Tockman, but something went wrong. Instead of slowing time, it... sped everything up. We thought maybe it was broken."

Mr. Tockman's eyes sparkled with understanding. "I see. Come, let's take a look."

He gestured for them to place the clock on his workbench, and they watched as he examined it closely. He ran his fingers over its face, feeling the crack that split across the glass, then gently tapped its hands, which were still frozen in place. His gaze softened as he held the clock, almost as if he were talking to an old friend.

"The clock isn't broken," he said finally, looking up at the family. "But it did respond to the way you used it."

Mrs. Baxter tilted her head, puzzled. "We were careful, Mr. Tockman. We remembered what you said about only using it when we truly needed it. It was a special day for us, and we thought the clock would help us make it last a little longer."

Mr. Tockman nodded, his expression both kind and serious. "I believe you. And it sounds like the day was indeed special. But sometimes, the clock senses when we're trying too hard to control time, rather than just letting it flow."

Max looked up, frowning thoughtfully. "So... you're saying the clock knew we were trying to stretch the day too much?"

Mr. Tockman nodded. "Exactly, Max. The clock is a tool, yes, but it also has its own way of understanding time. Its magic can only work properly when it senses a genuine need for extra time, not just a wish to make more time for fun or convenience. In fact, if the clock senses that you're leaning on it too much, it might react by doing the opposite of what you intended."

Emma's eyes widened, her curiosity piqued. "So... it's kind of like the clock has rules of its own?"

Mr. Tockman smiled warmly, nodding. "You could say that. Time, you see, is a balance. The clock's magic is meant to be a reminder, a gentle guide. It can't bend time for every special occasion, or it would lose its true purpose. When the clock senses that you're trying to create more time rather than appreciating the time you have, it sometimes responds by doing the opposite—speeding things up to remind you of that balance."

Mr. Baxter's expression softened as he listened. "So, it was our mistake for trying to make the day last longer?"

Mr. Tockman placed a comforting hand on the clock, smiling kindly. "Not a mistake, Mr. Baxter. Just a lesson. The clock is simply reminding you that some moments are meant to be experienced naturally, without any magic to make them last. It wants you to remember that true magic comes from how you spend your time, not from trying to create more of it."

Mrs. Baxter nodded, understanding dawning in her eyes. "We got so caught up in the idea of having more time that we forgot the importance of simply being in the moment."

Mr. Tockman gave a gentle nod. "Exactly. You see, when you focus too much on stretching time, you sometimes miss the joy of being fully present. The clock is there for the rare times when you truly need its help, but it's also there to remind you that life's most precious moments are often the ones we let unfold naturally."

Emma looked at the clock, her expression thoughtful. "So, if we want to use it, we have to be sure it's really needed, not just because we want more time?"

"Yes, Emma," Mr. Tockman said, a proud smile lighting up his face. "The clock's magic is meant to be used only when it can add something truly meaningful, something that couldn't be experienced any other way. Think of it as a friend who gently nudges you to see the beauty in ordinary time."

Max glanced at his parents, feeling both a sense of relief and newfound respect for the clock. "I guess we were asking too much of it. We weren't trying to, but we didn't really understand it."

Mr. Tockman chuckled, nodding. "It's all part of the learning process. The clock is here to help you, but it's also here to teach you about the nature of time itself. When you respect its magic and its limitations, it will serve you faithfully."

Mrs. Baxter reached out, gently placing a hand on the clock's face. "Thank you, Mr. Tockman. I think we understand now. We'll only use it when it's truly necessary—and we'll try to find the magic in ordinary time, too."

Mr. Tockman's eyes softened, and he carefully lifted the clock, handing it back to her. "I know you will. You have a good heart, Mrs.

Baxter, and I trust that you and your family will make the most of your time—both with and without the clock's help."

As they took the clock back into their hands, the family felt a renewed sense of appreciation for its quiet magic. They had come in seeking to "fix" the clock, but instead, they had gained a deeper understanding of its purpose, and a reminder of how precious time truly was.

As they left the shop, the family walked together, sharing a quiet moment of gratitude. They understood now that the clock was more than just a magical object—it was a guide, teaching them the importance of balance, mindfulness, and the beauty of being fully present.

At home, they returned the clock to its place on the shelf, glancing at it with a new sense of respect. They knew they wouldn't rely on it too often, but they also knew it would be there if they ever truly needed it, ready to help them slow down and savour a precious moment.

The clock sat quietly on the shelf, watching over them like a trusted friend. And from that day on, the Baxters carried with them a quiet promise: to let life unfold at its own pace, to find joy in ordinary moments, and to save the magic of the clock for times when they truly needed a little more time together.

Chapter 12: Grandma's Story

One rainy Saturday afternoon, Emma and Max were at home with their grandmother, who had come to stay with them for the weekend. Grandma Baxter was a warm, gentle woman with twinkling eyes and a laugh that filled the room with happiness. She had stories about almost everything, from her childhood to her travels, and Emma and Max loved hearing about the past from her perspective.

The rain pattered against the windows, and the three of them sat in the living room, nestled under cozy blankets with mugs of hot cocoa. The kids were hoping for another story, and they knew that once Grandma got started, her tales could keep them spellbound for hours.

"Grandma, can you tell us a story about when you were young?" Emma asked, her eyes bright with anticipation.

Grandma chuckled, taking a sip of her cocoa. "Oh, I've got plenty of those, sweetheart. But let me think... maybe I'll tell you a story about time."

Max raised an eyebrow, curious. "A story about time? Like, did you ever wish you had more time to do things?"

Grandma nodded, her gaze growing thoughtful. "Yes, Max, I did. When I was your age, I was always wishing I had more time for fun, more time to play with my friends or read my favorite books. But the older I got, the more I realized there was something I wished for even more than that."

Emma tilted her head, listening intently. "What was it, Grandma?"

Her grandmother's eyes softened as she looked at the two of them. "I wished for more time with the people I loved. Especially with my family."

Max and Emma exchanged glances, curious but also a little puzzled. They had never thought about time in quite that way.

"You see," Grandma continued, "when I was young, my parents were very busy. They loved me dearly, of course, but there were always things that had to be done—work, chores, and all the little responsibilities that come with being an adult. As I got older, I found myself wishing that we could slow down, just a little bit, so that we could spend more time together."

Emma thought about this, feeling a warm sympathy for her grandmother. "Did you ever get to slow down with them?"

Grandma Baxter sighed, her smile tinged with a touch of sadness. "Sometimes we did. Every now and then, my parents would take a day off, or we'd have a quiet evening together by the fire, telling stories and laughing. Those are some of my favorite memories. But even so, life seemed to rush by. It wasn't until I grew up and had children of my own that I really understood how precious those moments were."

She looked down at her hands, as if seeing her past in her palms. "If I could go back, I'd cherish every single one of those days a little more. I'd tell my younger self to hold on to those moments and not let them slip by so quickly. I think, deep down, that's why I love spending time with you two so much. It's like a second chance to appreciate what I have right here, right now."

The kids were silent for a moment, taking in their grandmother's words. Max looked at her, a question in his eyes. "Did you ever wish you could have a way to... slow down time? Like, if you had a magic clock or something?"

Grandma chuckled, but her eyes held a wistful light. "Oh, I would have loved a magic clock. Imagine how wonderful it would have been to pause everything, just so we could all sit together, talk, and laugh without worrying about the next thing on the list. But in a way, I think we all have our own little magic clocks."

Emma leaned forward, her curiosity piqued. "Really? How?"

Grandma smiled gently, reaching out to hold both of their hands. "You see, whenever we choose to be fully present in a moment—when we stop thinking about what we have to do next and just enjoy the people we're with—that's when we're making time feel a little slower.

It's like stretching out a second, or turning a few minutes into a memory that lasts a lifetime. That's a kind of magic, don't you think?"

Emma and Max nodded, understanding her words in a new way. They thought about all the times they'd laughed and played with their family, the moments they'd shared, and how each one felt like a little treasure. They knew, too, that their grandmother was right. When they focused on each other and enjoyed their time together, it felt richer and fuller, almost like time really was slowing down.

Grandma patted their hands and gave them a warm smile. "So remember, you two. You may have a magical clock, but the real magic is in how you spend your time. Even without the clock, you have the power to make each moment count, to turn ordinary days into something special just by being present."

Emma looked over at the clock on the shelf, feeling a sense of awe and gratitude. She and Max had always seen it as something that could give them more time, but now they understood that the clock was a reminder to appreciate the time they already had.

"Thank you, Grandma," Max said quietly, giving her a warm hug. "I think I get it now."

Grandma hugged him back, her face full of love and understanding. "Good. Because time has a funny way of moving quickly when we're not paying attention. But if you're present, if you really live in each moment, you'll find that you already have all the time you need."

Emma and Max sat quietly, holding on to their grandmother's words. They realized that while the clock was special, they didn't need magic to cherish their time together. In fact, their grandmother's wisdom was a kind of magic all on its own, reminding them to slow down and savour the moments that mattered most.

As they sat together, the rain pattered softly outside, creating a warm cocoon of quiet around them. They shared stories and laughter, each of them feeling a little closer, a little more grateful for the time they had to spend together.

That night, as the kids went to bed, they felt a renewed sense of appreciation for their family and the precious time they shared. They knew now that the clock's real magic wasn't just in bending time—it was in helping them see the beauty of the moments they had.

And as they drifted off to sleep, they carried with them their grandmother's words, a gentle reminder to cherish each day, to make the most of every moment, and to let their hearts be their guide in finding the true magic of time.

Chapter 13: An Unscheduled Adventure

It was a crisp, sunny Saturday morning, and the Baxter family was ready to settle into their usual weekend routine of chores, errands, and maybe a trip to the grocery store. However, as they sat together at breakfast, Mrs. Baxter looked out the window, her eyes catching the sunlight streaming through the trees, casting a warm, golden glow over everything.

"You know," she began, a thoughtful smile forming on her face, "it's such a beautiful day. Why don't we do something different?"

Emma and Max looked up, their eyes lighting up with curiosity. "Like what, Mom?" Max asked, already sensing the excitement in her tone.

Mrs. Baxter turned to Mr. Baxter, a twinkle in her eye. "Maybe we could have a family day at the park. Just spend some time together and enjoy the day."

Mr. Baxter smiled, nodding in agreement. "I think that sounds perfect. We could pack a picnic, bring a few games, and just let the day unfold without any plans."

Emma and Max grinned, thrilled at the idea of an unplanned day outdoors. They hurriedly helped pack snacks, a blanket, and a few games, filling the basket with everything they would need for a cozy outing. As they were gathering things, Emma spotted the old clock on the shelf, sitting quietly as if watching over them.

"Do you think we should bring it?" she asked, glancing at her parents. "Maybe... maybe it could help us make the day last a little longer."

Mr. Baxter considered this thoughtfully, nodding. "Why not? It seems like a special day, and we're not trying to stretch out any specific moment—we just want to enjoy whatever time we have."

With that, he carefully tucked the clock into the picnic basket, and they set off for the park, excitement bubbling in their hearts. As they strolled down the path, they felt the warmth of the autumn sun, the soft crunch of leaves underfoot, and the gentle breeze that carried with it the scent of pine and earth. Everything felt perfect, like the beginning of an unexpected adventure.

When they reached the park, they picked a spot beneath a large, spreading maple tree. Its leaves were a brilliant orange and red, casting a dappled, colorful shade over them. They spread out the blanket and settled in, unpacking sandwiches, fruit, and snacks, with the old clock sitting quietly in the center, like a silent guest.

As they began to eat, Emma noticed something strange and wonderful. The world around them seemed to grow softer, almost as if the clock were gently weaving its magic into the air. She looked up at the tree branches swaying above them, and it felt like they were moving in slow motion, each leaf catching the sunlight in a unique and beautiful way.

"Is it… is the clock working?" she whispered, glancing at Max, who looked around in awe.

"I think so," he replied, his voice hushed with wonder. "It's like everything's slowing down just a little."

Mrs. Baxter smiled, sensing the same gentle stillness in the air. "It's lovely, isn't it? It feels like we have all the time in the world to enjoy this moment."

They spent the next few hours lost in the beauty of the day. They lay back on the blanket, looking up at the tree branches and spotting shapes in the clouds that drifted lazily across the sky. Emma found a cloud that looked like a unicorn, while Max pointed out one shaped like a dragon, his excitement bubbling over as they watched the shapes slowly shift and change.

After lunch, Mr. Baxter suggested a game of catch. They took turns throwing a small rubber ball, laughing as they chased after each other and occasionally flopped onto the grass, catching their breath. Each moment felt like it stretched out, allowing them to savour every laugh, every playful leap, every shared glance of joy.

At one point, Mrs. Baxter found herself sitting on the blanket, watching her family run and laugh in the soft, glowing light. She placed her hand gently on the clock, feeling its steady warmth, and a deep gratitude filled her heart. This unscheduled day, this simple outing, was turning into one of the most beautiful memories she'd ever experienced.

Emma and Max ran back to the blanket, cheeks flushed and eyes shining with happiness. They plopped down beside their mother, out of breath but filled with joy.

"This is the best day ever," Emma said, her voice filled with contentment. "It feels like it's lasting forever, but in a really good way."

Max nodded, looking around at the trees, the sunlight, and his family. "It's like we're inside a perfect moment. I don't even want to think about anything else."

Mr. Baxter joined them, settling down on the blanket and pulling his family close. "That's the beauty of a day like this," he said softly. "Sometimes, when we don't try to plan every detail, the best memories happen naturally."

They sat together, soaking in the peace and beauty of the afternoon, each of them feeling the magic of time slowing just enough to let them truly appreciate each other. The clock seemed to hum gently beside them, as if sharing their joy and holding them in this unhurried space.

As the sun began to dip lower in the sky, casting long, golden shadows across the park, they knew it was time to head home. They packed up slowly, savouring each last moment of their day, reluctant to let it end. As they walked back, the air felt different, as if the clock had gifted them not just with more time, but with a deeper understanding of how precious time together really was.

That evening, back at home, they placed the clock carefully back on the shelf, sharing a silent moment of gratitude. Emma looked up at her parents, her heart full. "Thank you for today. It was... magical."

Mrs. Baxter kissed her on the forehead. "It was magical because we let it be. We didn't try to make it perfect; we just enjoyed what was in front of us."

Max gave the clock one last glance, smiling to himself. "I think it helped us see how special time can be when we just let it happen."

That night, as they all went to bed, each of them carried a piece of that perfect day with them—a quiet reminder that sometimes, the best adventures are the ones we don't plan, the ones that unfold naturally and create memories we'll hold close for a lifetime.

And as the house settled into silence, the clock sat quietly on the shelf, its cracked face catching the soft glow of the moonlight. It had done its work, slowing time just enough for the Baxter family to see the magic in each other and the world around them, leaving them with a memory they would cherish forever.

Chapter 14: Savouring Small Moments

It had been a busy week, filled with school, work, and the usual flurry of activities. By the time Friday evening rolled around, the Baxter family was ready for a quiet night at home. Mrs. Baxter had decided to make a family favorite—spaghetti and meatballs with warm garlic bread, and the kitchen was filled with the delicious aroma of simmering tomato sauce and baking bread.

Emma and Max set the table together, each feeling a warm anticipation for dinner. They loved Friday nights, when they could all sit down together without the rush of homework or other distractions. As they laid out the silverware and glasses, Emma glanced over at the old clock on the shelf, her heart filling with a sudden thought.

"Max," she whispered, catching his attention. "Do you think we could use the clock tonight? Just to make this dinner last a little longer?"

Max looked over at the clock, nodding slowly as he took in her idea. "Yeah... we're always in a hurry during dinner, and sometimes it feels like it goes by too fast. It'd be nice to slow down, just this once, and really enjoy it."

Emma grinned, happy that he understood. They both knew this wasn't just any meal—it was a chance to savour their family time, to appreciate each moment as it came. She carefully picked up the clock from the shelf and placed it on the dining table, close to where everyone could see it.

When their parents joined them at the table, they noticed the clock and exchanged curious glances. "What's this?" Mrs. Baxter asked, smiling as she looked from Emma to Max.

Emma smiled shyly. "We thought... maybe we could use the clock tonight. Just to make dinner last a little longer."

Max added, his face earnest, "We love Friday dinners, and it'd be nice to have a little extra time to enjoy it, without feeling like we're in a rush."

Mr. and Mrs. Baxter shared a warm look, touched by their children's thoughtfulness. Mrs. Baxter reached out and placed a gentle hand on the clock. "I think that's a beautiful idea," she said, her voice filled with warmth. "Let's make this a dinner to remember."

They all held hands around the table, pausing to appreciate the moment. Then, as if in response to their shared wish, a gentle warmth spread from the clock, wrapping around the table like a soft, invisible blanket. The usual rush of time seemed to slow, softening the edges of each moment, and they each felt a quiet sense of calm settle over them.

As they began to eat, everything felt heightened—the aromas, the tastes, the sounds of laughter. Emma took her first bite of spaghetti, marveling at the rich flavour of the sauce, the way the spices danced on her tongue. She had eaten this meal countless times, but tonight, it tasted different, like she was experiencing every ingredient for the first time.

"Wow, Mom," she said, savouring each bite. "This is the best spaghetti I've ever tasted!"

Mrs. Baxter laughed, her eyes twinkling. "I think you say that every time, Emma. But thank you."

Max reached for the garlic bread, tearing off a warm, buttery piece and taking a slow bite. "It really does taste better tonight," he said thoughtfully. "It's like we can taste everything—like every bite has a story."

They all laughed, and the sound of their voices seemed to linger in the air a little longer than usual, filling the room with warmth. The meal became a symphony of small, perfect moments—Mrs. Baxter pouring juice, Mr. Baxter telling a funny story from work, Emma and Max giggling at the spaghetti sauce that kept landing on their faces no matter how careful they tried to be.

As the evening unfolded, the family found themselves talking about things they hadn't discussed in a long time. They shared stories, remembered little moments from the past, and even dreamed about future family adventures. There was no rush, no need to move on to the next task—only the simple joy of being together.

At one point, Mr. Baxter held up his glass, his face thoughtful. "You know, we don't always have to do something big or special for it to be meaningful. Sometimes, just sitting down together, sharing a meal like this, is the most special thing of all."

Mrs. Baxter nodded, raising her glass to join him. "To savouring the small moments," she said, smiling at each of them. "Because they're the ones that make life beautiful."

Emma and Max raised their glasses, grinning. "To small moments!" they echoed, feeling a rush of warmth and gratitude.

As they continued their meal, they found themselves paying closer attention to each other, noticing the little things they might usually miss. Emma watched the way her dad's eyes crinkled when he laughed, and Max noticed the way his mom's face softened as she listened to them share their stories. Even the clinking of their forks and the soft murmur of their voices became part of the memory they were creating together.

Eventually, as the last bites were eaten and the plates were empty, they all sat back, feeling full and content. The magic of the clock had stretched the dinner into something more—a moment of closeness, of laughter, of quiet appreciation for the family they had.

As the evening wound down, Emma gently placed the clock back on the shelf, looking at it with a newfound respect. She had always thought of it as a way to make big, special days last longer, but tonight, she realized its magic could also make the small, everyday moments feel just as meaningful.

Max gave her a soft smile, sensing her thoughts. "It really was perfect, wasn't it?"

Emma nodded. "It was. I think I understand now. We don't need the clock all the time, just for moments like these—moments we want to remember forever."

Their parents joined them, sharing a quiet, contented smile. Mrs. Baxter wrapped her arms around them both, pulling them close. "Thank you, Emma and Max. You reminded us of something very important tonight. Sometimes, the best moments aren't planned or fancy. They're the simple, everyday moments we share with each other."

With that, they turned out the lights and went to bed, each of them feeling a quiet joy that lingered like the warmth of a candle. The magic of the evening had been in its simplicity, in the way they had slowed down, looked at each other, and shared a meal as though it were the most special feast in the world.

And as the house grew still, the clock sat on the shelf, quietly watching over them, its cracked face gleaming softly in the moonlight. It had given them the gift of time—not by adding more minutes, but by showing them how to savour the ones they already had.

Chapter 15: Lessons at School

It was a chilly Monday morning, and Max was feeling the familiar flutter of nerves as he walked into his classroom. Today was test day, and he'd spent the entire weekend studying for it. But even with all his preparation, he couldn't shake the feeling of anxiety that crept into his stomach as he thought about the test questions waiting for him.

As he took his seat, Max glanced down at his backpack, where he'd carefully tucked the magical clock. He'd brought it with him, thinking that maybe, just maybe, the clock's magic could help him slow down and focus during the test. After all, it had made family moments last longer, allowing him and his family to savour every second. Maybe it could help him make the test feel less overwhelming, giving him the time he needed to think through each question.

Max waited until the teacher handed out the test and then took a deep breath, quietly slipping the clock out of his backpack and placing it in his lap under his desk. He gently pressed his hand to the clock's face, hoping to feel the familiar warmth, the calm that usually came when the clock's magic began to work.

"Please, just give me a little extra time," he whispered, closing his eyes.

He waited, expecting the clock to hum softly in his hands, expecting to feel the minutes stretching out, allowing him to slow down and focus on each question without the usual rush of test anxiety. But instead, the clock remained cold and still, its hands as unmoving as ever.

Max frowned, puzzled. He tried holding it a little closer, concentrating harder, silently urging it to work its magic. But nothing happened. Time continued to tick on as usual, the classroom clock ticking steadily in the background. The test questions were still waiting, the minutes still slipping by at their normal pace.

A sinking feeling crept over him as he realized that the clock's magic wasn't working. He couldn't make it slow down time just because he wanted a little extra help with his test. For the first time, he wondered if he'd misunderstood the clock's purpose.

Max glanced around at his classmates, all of whom were focused on their own tests, and then back down at the clock in his lap. He felt a pang of disappointment mixed with frustration. Why wasn't the clock helping him? Hadn't he needed extra time? Wasn't that what it was for?

But as he looked at the clock, a quiet understanding began to settle over him. Mr. Tockman had always said the clock was meant for moments that mattered, moments shared with family. It was a gift that allowed them to treasure their time together—not a tool for personal convenience, and certainly not a shortcut for everyday tasks.

Max took a deep breath, realizing that he'd been trying to use the clock's magic for something it wasn't meant to do. The clock wasn't there to make things easier or to fix small problems; it was there to help his family create meaningful memories, to slow down and appreciate each other. Using it in the middle of a school test felt wrong, like he was trying to take advantage of something special and sacred.

With a sigh, he placed the clock carefully back into his backpack, closing the zipper and resolving to face the test on his own. He realized that part of what made the clock's magic so powerful was that it was limited to family moments. It was a reminder of what mattered most—not achieving perfect scores or fixing everyday problems, but cherishing the time they had together.

Max looked down at his test, feeling a surprising sense of calm wash over him. The clock may not be able to help him with this challenge, but he had prepared, and he knew he could do his best. He picked up his pencil and began to work, focusing on each question and letting go of his worries. Even without the clock's magic, he found that he was able to focus more than he'd expected, relying on his own preparation and determination.

When the bell rang to signal the end of the test, Max felt a surge of relief. He'd done his best, and that was enough. As he walked out of the classroom, he felt a new respect for the clock, understanding now that its magic wasn't something to be used lightly or for personal gain.

That evening, back at home, Max gathered his family in the living room and told them about what had happened at school.

"I tried to use the clock during my test," he admitted, feeling a little sheepish. "I thought it could help me focus, but it didn't work. I think it only works when we're together as a family."

Mrs. Baxter smiled, placing a gentle hand on his shoulder. "That makes sense, Max. The clock was given to us as a family gift, to help us appreciate our time together. I think it knew that using it for a test wasn't quite the same."

Mr. Baxter nodded, his expression thoughtful. "It sounds like you've learned something important. The clock's magic is special because it's meant to bring us closer, to help us cherish our moments as a family. When we try to use it for things outside of that purpose, it reminds us that some things are meant to be done on our own."

Emma, who had been listening quietly, reached out and hugged Max. "I'm proud of you, Max. And I think it's really cool that you figured out the clock's magic is about family. That makes it even more special."

Max smiled, feeling a warm sense of pride. He had learned a valuable lesson, one that he knew he would carry with him. The clock wasn't just a magical object; it was a reminder of his family, of the moments they shared, and of the love that bound them together.

That night, as Max went to bed, he glanced at the clock on the shelf, feeling grateful for the lesson it had taught him. He understood now that the clock's magic was something rare and precious, something meant to be treasured and used wisely. And as he drifted off to sleep, he knew that the true magic lay not in slowing down time for every challenge, but in making the most of the time he had, both with his family and on his own.

The clock sat quietly, its face glowing softly in the moonlight, as if nodding in agreement. It had done its job, guiding Max to a deeper understanding of what really mattered.

Chapter 16: Friends or Family?

It was a bright, sunny afternoon, and Emma and Max had invited a few friends over to play in the backyard. The day was filled with laughter, games, and the kind of joy that only comes from spending time with friends. They played tag, built forts with blankets and branches, and even pretended the backyard was a hidden jungle filled with secret treasures. For Emma and Max, it was one of those perfect days that felt like it would last forever.

But as the sun began to sink lower in the sky, casting long shadows across the yard, they realized the day was slipping away faster than they'd hoped. Soon, their friends would have to go home, and the fun would come to an end. Max exchanged a glance with Emma, both of them feeling a pang of disappointment.

"I wish we could make this day last longer," Max murmured, glancing back at their friends, who were still laughing and playing in the fading sunlight.

Emma nodded, her gaze drifting to the house where the clock sat quietly on the living room shelf. She could almost feel its presence, as if it were watching over them even from afar. "What if... what if we used the clock?" she whispered, feeling a thrill of excitement. "Just a little bit, to make the day last a bit longer. It would be amazing to have extra time with our friends."

Max looked uncertain but tempted. "I don't know... Mr. Tockman did say the clock is meant for family. But it's just this once, right? Our friends are practically like family."

They both stood there, torn between their longing to keep playing with their friends and the knowledge that the clock's magic was something rare and special. They felt a strong urge to make the day last longer, to stretch out this perfect moment of friendship and laughter. After all, what could it hurt? They reasoned that it was only one day, and surely the clock would understand.

After a brief pause, they dashed into the house, grabbing the clock from its place on the shelf. They carried it carefully back to the backyard, holding it between them as they looked at each other, hearts pounding.

"Alright," Emma said, glancing at the clock with anticipation. "Just a little bit, so we can have more time with our friends. Then we'll put it back, and no one will even know."

They placed the clock in the center of their gathering, hoping to feel the familiar warmth, the gentle slowing of time that would allow them to play just a little bit longer. But as they waited, nothing happened. The clock sat silently, its hands unmoving, its face reflecting the evening light without the faintest sign of magic.

Max frowned, touching the clock's face. "Why isn't it working? It's like it doesn't... want to help."

Emma felt a sinking feeling. She remembered Mr. Tockman's words, how he'd explained that the clock was a family gift, meant to create memories together with their loved ones. "Maybe... maybe it's because we're not using it with our family. Maybe it can't work for anything else."

Max sighed, disappointment flickering across his face. "So, it only works when it's all of us together as a family. Not with friends."

They both looked at their friends playing nearby, feeling a mixture of sadness and understanding. The clock's magic wasn't for every special day, and it wasn't for just anyone. It was meant to deepen the time they spent with family, to make those moments truly unforgettable. They both realized that using it for anything else would take away from the very reason it was special.

Emma picked up the clock, holding it gently. "I think... I think we should put it back. It's not right to try and use it for something it's not meant for."

Max nodded, his face thoughtful. "Yeah, you're right. Our friends are important, but family time is different. It's like... that's what the clock was created for."

They carefully returned the clock to the shelf, feeling a new sense of respect for it. They had almost misused its magic, but now they understood its purpose more clearly. The clock was for family—those moments when they were together, sharing love, laughter, and memories that couldn't be created with anyone else.

When they returned to the yard, the day had grown shorter, and their friends were getting ready to head home. Emma and Max joined them, enjoying the last few minutes, but this time with a new perspective. They knew now that their family time held a special kind of magic, one that didn't need the clock to be memorable.

That evening, after their friends had left, Emma and Max sat down with their parents and shared what had happened. They admitted how they had wanted to use the clock to make their time with friends last longer, and how they had learned that the clock was meant for family moments only.

Mrs. Baxter listened, her face warm with understanding. "I'm proud of both of you for recognizing that. Friends are wonderful, and we'll always have special times with them, but family is something unique. The clock is a reminder of that—of the moments we share that no one else can replace."

Mr. Baxter nodded, his voice thoughtful. "The clock's magic isn't just in slowing down time. It's in helping us see the value of our time together as a family. When we're together, we create memories that no one else can—memories that are uniquely ours."

Emma and Max shared a glance, feeling grateful for their family and the lessons the clock had taught them. They realized that the true magic of the clock wasn't just in extending moments but in helping them understand what made those moments special. Friends would come and go, but family would always be there, sharing moments that only they could truly understand and cherish.

Later that night, as Emma lay in bed, she thought about the clock and all the things it had taught her. She knew now that family was its own kind of magic, one that didn't need extra time or special powers to be meaningful. She felt a quiet pride in knowing she and Max had learned something valuable—that their family time was precious, and the clock was there to remind them of that, nothing more.

The clock sat quietly on the shelf, its cracked face glinting in the moonlight, a silent guardian of their family moments. And as the house grew still, it seemed to glow with a soft, quiet light, as if pleased that its magic had been understood and appreciated once again.

Part 4: The Clock's Consequence
Chapter 17: The Birthday Dilemma

Excitement buzzed in the Baxter household as they prepared for a very special occasion—Mr. Baxter's birthday. The whole family had been planning the celebration for weeks, filling the day with Mr. Baxter's favorite activities: a pancake breakfast, an afternoon at the park, and a small party with cake, presents, and laughter. Emma and Max had even planned a few surprise games to make the day extra memorable.

The morning began with pancakes, laughter, and presents, and the house was filled with the happy chaos that only a family celebration could bring. By the time they gathered in the living room for cake, Emma and Max exchanged a hopeful glance.

"Do you think we could use the clock today?" Emma whispered to Max as they watched their dad blow out the candles. "It's Dad's birthday, and it would be amazing to make the party last a little longer."

Max nodded, sharing her excitement. "Yeah! We could use the clock just this once, to make the day extra special for him. After all, birthdays only come once a year."

The idea grew in both of their minds, and after the cake had been cut and the first slice was served, they approached their parents with the suggestion.

"Mom, Dad," Max began, his voice filled with enthusiasm, "we were thinking... since it's your birthday, maybe we could use the clock to make the party last a bit longer. You know, so we can enjoy every moment."

Mr. Baxter looked at his kids, a smile touching his lips. "I appreciate that, Max. But do you think the clock is meant for something like this?"

Emma and Max exchanged glances, both of them hesitant but hopeful. "It's a family celebration, after all," Emma said. "And Mr. Tockman said the clock was for family time, right?"

Mrs. Baxter looked thoughtful. "Why don't we stop by Tockman's Clocks and ask Mr. Tockman himself? He might be able to tell us if a birthday celebration is a good reason to use the clock."

Emma and Max nodded eagerly, and within minutes, they were on their way to the clock shop, carrying the clock carefully with them. The afternoon sun bathed the cobbled street in golden light, making everything feel a little more magical, as if the day were already special enough on its own.

When they entered the shop, the familiar chime sounded above the door, and Mr. Tockman looked up from his workbench with a warm smile. "Ah, the Baxter family! And I see you've brought our magical friend with you. How can I help today?"

Emma stepped forward, holding the clock in her arms. "Mr. Tockman, it's Dad's birthday, and we were wondering if maybe... maybe we could use the clock to make the party last a little longer."

Max nodded enthusiastically. "Just for today! We thought it might be okay since it's a family celebration."

Mr. Tockman listened with a gentle smile, his eyes twinkling with understanding. He took the clock from Emma, turning it slowly in his hands, as if he were considering their request. Finally, he looked up, his gaze kind but serious.

"I understand why you'd want to make today last longer. Birthdays are indeed special, and it's wonderful that you want to savour every moment with your family." He paused, his expression thoughtful. "But the clock isn't meant to be used for every celebration or occasion. It's a tool to help you when time feels especially precious—not just because you're having fun or want to keep the party going."

Emma's face fell slightly. "So... it's not really meant for birthdays?"

Mr. Tockman shook his head gently. "Birthdays are wonderful, but they're meant to happen once a year, just as they are. Part of what makes them special is that they come and go, leaving behind warm memories. If you tried to make every fun day or every birthday last longer, the magic of the clock would start to feel ordinary, and you'd lose the sense of wonder that it's meant to bring."

Max bit his lip, thinking over Mr. Tockman's words. "So, the clock isn't just for making good moments last longer. It's more for... the moments we can't get back?"

Mr. Tockman nodded, pleased. "Exactly, Max. The clock is a reminder to cherish the truly important times, like those rare moments when you feel time slipping by too quickly. It's not meant to be used like a toy, even on special days."

Emma looked at the clock, her heart full of understanding. "So, if we used it every time we wanted to make a fun day last, we'd start to forget why the clock is so special."

Mr. Tockman placed a hand on her shoulder, his eyes warm with pride. "You've got it, Emma. Sometimes, the most magical days are the ones that end just as they are meant to, leaving us with beautiful memories rather than trying to make every moment last forever."

Mrs. Baxter reached out and gently took the clock from Mr. Tockman, smiling at her children. "Why don't we let today be one of those special memories we hold in our hearts? We'll enjoy it just as it is, without using the clock. That way, we can save its magic for a time when we really, truly need it."

Emma and Max nodded, feeling a new sense of respect for the clock. They realized that they didn't need its magic to make the day special—it was already magical simply because they were together as a family, sharing laughter, love, and memories.

"Thank you, Mr. Tockman," Max said, a smile on his face. "We understand now."

Mr. Tockman returned the smile, nodding approvingly. "I'm glad to hear it. Remember, magic is most powerful when it's rare. And sometimes, simply appreciating a moment for what it is can be the most magical thing of all."

The family left the shop with the clock carefully tucked away, their hearts lighter and their minds clearer. When they returned home, they continued the celebration without any extra magic, just the joy of being together and sharing laughter over birthday cake and stories.

As the evening drew to a close, they gathered around Mr. Baxter to share one last toast. "To family, and to making each moment count," he said, raising his glass with a smile.

"To making each moment count!" Emma and Max echoed, clinking their glasses together.

That night, as they went to bed, Emma and Max reflected on what Mr. Tockman had told them. They realized that the clock's true gift was in helping them understand the value of time, to cherish it without trying to control it. Birthdays, they knew now, were meant to be savoured for what they were, not stretched out by magic. And knowing that made the memories even sweeter.

The clock sat quietly on the shelf, a silent guardian of their time together. It had taught them a new lesson, one they would carry with them for birthdays, celebrations, and everyday moments alike. And as the house settled into peaceful quiet, they knew that the best memories were the ones that stayed with them, lingering like the warmth of a candle long after the day was done.

Chapter 18: Breaking the Rules

Emma and Max had done their best to respect the clock's magic. After Mr. Tockman's reminder, they understood the importance of using it sparingly, to make only truly special moments last longer. But as time went by, they couldn't resist the allure of the clock's magic. The idea of having more time for fun, for games, or even to avoid a chore or two was just too tempting.

One rainy afternoon, while their parents were busy with work, Emma glanced at the clock on the shelf. She knew it was supposed to be reserved for family moments, but she couldn't help but wonder what it would be like to use the clock just a little bit more.

"What if we used it, just for today?" she suggested to Max, her eyes gleaming with excitement. "It's not like we're asking for a lot—just a few extra hours to play."

Max looked hesitant but couldn't deny the temptation. "It would be nice to have more time for fun. We're always so rushed with homework and everything else."

They glanced at the clock, sharing a mischievous smile. Ignoring their better judgment, they took it down from the shelf, cradling it in their hands as they whispered their wish: "Just a little more time, so we can play longer."

At first, everything seemed to go smoothly. They felt the familiar warmth of the clock, and soon, time seemed to stretch around them, allowing them extra hours of unhurried play. But as they continued, it became harder and harder to resist using the clock for more things.

A few days later, they tried it again—this time, to make their evening snack last a bit longer, so they could keep chatting. Then they used it once more to extend the weekend, hoping to avoid the rush of Monday morning. Each time, they felt the clock's gentle hum, its magic allowing them more time for whatever they wanted.

But gradually, strange things began to happen.

One evening, as they sat down to dinner with their parents, Emma glanced at the clock on the wall, noticing that the second hand was moving unusually fast, as if rushing through each minute. She blinked, startled. "Max, look at the clock. It's going too quickly."

Max looked up, frowning. "That's weird. Do you think...?"

He trailed off as the clock on the wall seemed to slow down abruptly, its second hand now ticking once every few seconds instead of its usual pace. The minutes stretched out in a strange, irregular rhythm, speeding up, then slowing down, as if time itself were getting confused.

They exchanged worried glances, a sense of unease creeping over them.

The next day, things grew even stranger. In the middle of the school day, time seemed to skip altogether, with entire minutes vanishing as if they'd been erased. Emma glanced at her watch, noticing that five minutes had passed in the blink of an eye. At home, Max found himself in a similar situation; one moment he was brushing his teeth, and the next, he was already in bed, as if he'd missed the time in between.

The unusual effects continued over the next several days. They couldn't predict when time would speed up, slow down, or skip altogether. At first, it had been fun to make their days last longer, but now it was beginning to feel eerie and unsettling.

"I think we've messed something up," Max whispered to Emma one evening as they sat on the edge of her bed, both of them feeling the weight of their actions. "Time isn't acting right. It's like it's... broken."

Emma's face paled as she clutched the clock tightly, worry flickering in her eyes. "Do you think we used the clock too much?"

Max nodded slowly. "We ignored what Mr. Tockman said. We broke the rules."

The realization hit them both hard. By overusing the clock, they had disrupted the very balance of time around them. What had once been a gentle, magical gift was now creating chaos, like a river overflowing its banks and flooding everything in its path. The clock wasn't meant to be used whenever they wanted, and now they were paying the price.

Desperate to fix what they had done, they decided to visit Mr. Tockman the very next day. They carefully wrapped the clock and carried it back to his shop, their hearts heavy with regret. The familiar chime over the door sounded as they entered, but today, the shop felt different—more serious, almost sombre.

Mr. Tockman looked up from his workbench, his eyes soft with understanding but filled with concern as he took in the sight of the clock in their hands.

"Ah, I see," he murmured, nodding slowly. "You've discovered what happens when the clock's magic is misused."

Emma's eyes filled with tears. "We're so sorry, Mr. Tockman. We didn't mean to cause trouble. We just... we wanted a little more time, just to make things last longer."

Mr. Tockman nodded kindly, motioning for them to place the clock on his workbench. "I understand, Emma. And it's natural to want more time—it's something we all wish for. But the clock's magic isn't like an ordinary tool. It's delicate, and it relies on balance. When used too often or without thought, it begins to lose its sense of purpose. That's why things have been going haywire."

Max looked down, ashamed. "We thought we could just use it whenever we wanted. But now I see that it's only meant for really special moments."

Mr. Tockman placed a gentle hand on Max's shoulder. "You've learned an important lesson. Magic isn't just about making things last; it's about understanding why we cherish those moments in the first place. When you try to control time too much, you lose the very magic you're trying to keep."

Emma wiped her eyes, looking up at Mr. Tockman with a hopeful expression. "Can it be fixed? Can time go back to normal?"

Mr. Tockman nodded, his gaze reassuring. "Yes, it can. But you'll have to be very careful going forward. I'll help reset the clock's magic, but it will take time to recover. From now on, remember that this clock isn't a toy or a convenience. It's a gift meant to remind you to cherish the moments that naturally unfold."

He carefully placed his hands on the clock, murmuring a few quiet words as he gently adjusted its hands. Emma and Max watched as the clock glowed softly, its warmth returning in a steady, peaceful rhythm. They felt a wave of calm wash over them, as if the clock's balance was being restored.

Finally, Mr. Tockman handed the clock back to them, his expression kind but firm. "This clock will work properly again, but only if you treat it with respect. Use it sparingly, and only when time truly needs to slow down. Trust me, the most magical moments in life aren't the ones we try to control—they're the ones that happen naturally."

Emma and Max nodded solemnly, feeling the weight of his words. They realized now that the clock's power wasn't just in extending time; it was in teaching them to appreciate time for what it was—a precious, fleeting gift that shouldn't be taken for granted.

As they walked home, they felt a renewed sense of responsibility. They placed the clock carefully back on the shelf, vowing to respect its magic and only use it when it was truly needed.

That night, as they went to bed, Emma and Max felt a quiet peace settle over them. They knew that from now on, they would treasure their family moments for what they were, without trying to stretch or change them. The clock had taught them a powerful lesson, one they would never forget: that time was most beautiful when it was left to flow on its own, each moment a gift in its own right.

The clock sat quietly on the shelf, its face glowing softly in the moonlight. And as the house settled into peaceful silence, the Baxters knew that they had finally learned to respect the magic that had been entrusted to them.

Chapter 19: Lost in Fast-Forward

Emma and Max had promised themselves to use the clock sparingly after their conversation with Mr. Tockman. They'd been shaken by the experience of time slipping out of control, and they understood now that the clock's magic was not something to be taken lightly. But even with their best intentions, the habit of wanting "just a little more time" was hard to break.

A few weeks after the birthday party, on a regular school night, Emma found herself wishing she could speed through her homework so she'd have more time to relax. She mentioned it to Max, who, feeling equally restless, shrugged and said, "Maybe we could use the clock just once more. I mean, we wouldn't need a lot of extra time—just a little."

They took the clock down from the shelf and, hoping for a boost of energy, whispered their wish to make time move faster just for their homework. But instead of helping, the clock's magic spun wildly out of control. They felt a sudden pull, like being swept up by a strong current, and in the blink of an eye, they were catapulted into a dizzying world where everything was moving far too quickly.

The next day, they woke up to find that time seemed to be racing ahead in a way that was both strange and unsettling. Emma looked at the kitchen clock, blinking in confusion as the hands spun rapidly. They had barely started breakfast when it felt like the morning was slipping by in a blur. The sun rose higher, moving across the sky at an unnatural speed, and before they knew it, the school day was over, and they were back at home.

"What... what just happened?" Max asked, his eyes wide with confusion as he tried to make sense of the day that seemed to have vanished in an instant.

Emma shook her head, bewildered. "It felt like we skipped right through everything! I don't even remember most of today."

And it didn't stop there. Over the next few days, everything seemed to be stuck on fast-forward, as if they were hurtling through time without being able to slow down. Days blurred into nights, and entire conversations slipped by without them fully noticing. They missed little moments with their friends, stories in class, and even shared family dinners that usually brought them comfort.

One evening, they found themselves sitting at the dinner table with their parents, who were sharing a story from their day. But before they could fully take it in, the story was over, and their parents were already clearing the dishes, moving on to the next part of their routine. Emma and Max exchanged worried glances, realizing that they couldn't even remember what the story had been about.

"I feel like we're missing everything," Emma whispered to Max as they retreated to their rooms that night, her voice tinged with sadness. "I can barely remember what anyone said or did. It's like... like everything's slipping by too fast."

Max nodded, the weight of their predicament settling heavily on his shoulders. "This is horrible. It's like we're trapped in a world where nothing lasts long enough to matter."

And with each passing day, they felt the sting of lost moments even more sharply. They missed out on Emma's art project presentation, a surprise celebration for a friend's birthday, and little family conversations that once made them feel connected. The days blurred together, and even the weekends raced by in a haze. It was as though the very essence of time—the warmth of each moment, the beauty of each shared laugh—was slipping through their fingers like sand.

One evening, after yet another dinner that felt like a blink, Emma sat down and buried her face in her hands. "I can't keep doing this, Max. I miss everything—the time with Mom and Dad, the talks we used to have, even the little things, like just sitting down and feeling like we're here."

Max placed a comforting hand on her shoulder, his own face drawn with regret. "I know, Emma. I feel it too. It's like we've been... erased from our own lives. Everything's going by so quickly that we can't even enjoy it. I think this is what Mr. Tockman was trying to warn us about."

Emma nodded, wiping away a tear. "We broke the rules. We used the clock to try to make everything easier, and now it feels like we're being punished by missing everything that matters."

Desperate to fix what they'd done, they took the clock down from the shelf one more time, determined to go back to Mr. Tockman and explain everything. They made their way to Tockman's Clocks, hoping that he could help them restore the balance they'd disrupted.

When they entered the shop, Mr. Tockman was waiting for them, his expression calm but serious. He seemed to sense the heaviness they were carrying, and he motioned for them to sit down.

"We didn't listen, Mr. Tockman," Max admitted, his voice trembling. "We overused the clock, and now time's going too fast. We're missing everything that matters, and it feels awful."

Emma added, her voice filled with regret, "It's like... like we're no longer part of our own lives. Every important moment is slipping by before we can even feel it."

Mr. Tockman looked at them, his expression filled with understanding and compassion. "You've learned a difficult lesson, haven't you? Time is precious precisely because it moves forward, because each moment is unique and irreplaceable. When you try to control time, you end up losing the very essence of what makes it meaningful."

He held up the clock, his voice gentle but firm. "This clock was meant to remind you to savour your moments, not to avoid them. When you overuse it, time reacts by racing ahead, almost like it's trying to catch up. The magic of the clock isn't about making things easier or longer; it's about teaching you to appreciate the time you have."

Emma and Max nodded, fully understanding the truth in his words. They had taken their time together for granted, using the clock to make things last instead of appreciating each moment for what it was. And in doing so, they'd lost sight of the beauty of simply being present.

"Can it be fixed?" Max asked, his voice small. "Can we go back to experiencing time the way we're supposed to?"

Mr. Tockman smiled kindly, nodding. "Yes, but it will take time and patience. The clock's magic will reset itself, but only if you promise to honour its purpose. From now on, treat each moment with respect, and remember that it's the natural flow of time that makes life meaningful."

They each took a deep breath, feeling the weight of their responsibility. Together, they placed the clock back on the shelf in Mr. Tockman's shop, where he assured them it would stay for a few days to fully recover its balance. Only once they had truly let go of the urge to control time would he allow them to take it home again.

As they walked home, Emma and Max felt a quiet peace settle over them. Without the clock's magic, they knew they would need to approach each day with a renewed sense of mindfulness and gratitude. They couldn't control time, but they could choose to appreciate it.

The next few days felt strange at first, as they adjusted to letting go of the clock's magic. But soon, they found that each moment felt richer, each conversation more meaningful. And when they finally returned to Mr. Tockman's shop to bring the clock back home, they did so with a new understanding of its purpose.

From that day on, Emma and Max carried a deep respect for the natural flow of time. They no longer tried to control it or stretch it out, but instead, they allowed each moment to unfold as it was meant to. And as they looked at the clock on the shelf, they felt a quiet gratitude for the lesson it had taught them—a lesson that would stay with them for the rest of their lives.

Chapter 20: A Family Meeting

It had been a week since they'd left the clock in Mr. Tockman's shop, and life at the Baxter home had begun to return to its natural rhythm. Without the clock's magic, the family experienced the usual rush of school, work, and daily routines, but there was a difference this time. They were all a little more mindful, paying attention to each other, and noticing the small, precious details they'd once taken for granted.

One Friday evening, as they gathered around the dinner table, Mr. Baxter looked at each of them, sensing the importance of the moment. He cleared his throat, giving them a gentle smile.

"Why don't we have a family meeting?" he suggested. "Let's talk about the clock, what we've learned, and where we go from here."

Emma and Max shared a glance, nodding eagerly. They had both been thinking about the clock since they left it with Mr. Tockman, and they had their own reflections and regrets to share. They each carried a quiet understanding now, a sense of how the clock's magic had affected their family time.

Mrs. Baxter looked at them warmly, her gaze soft and patient. "Why don't you start, Emma? What's on your mind?"

Emma took a deep breath, thinking back to all the times they'd used the clock for little things—extra playtime, extended dinners, even help with homework. "I think... I think we started using the clock to avoid things," she said slowly, looking around the table. "Like, when we didn't want to rush or when we wanted more time to do something fun. But instead of just enjoying the time we had, we tried to make every moment last longer."

Max nodded, picking up where she left off. "Yeah, and I guess we got carried away. The more we used it, the more it felt like we needed it, even for things that weren't that important. We thought it was helping, but really... it was like we started to depend on it."

Mr. Baxter gave a thoughtful nod, resting his chin on his hand. "I agree, Max. I think there were times when we were so focused on trying to make things last that we forgot to just be together. We were trying to control every moment instead of enjoying it."

Mrs. Baxter leaned forward, her eyes gentle and understanding. "And because of that, I think we've missed out on real time together. Moments that were naturally meaningful, without the magic. It's easy to see now that the magic was more of a distraction than a help."

Emma and Max exchanged another glance, feeling the weight of her words. They had never intended for the clock to take away from their family time, but somehow, that was exactly what had happened. Each of them had been so focused on using the clock to make things "better" that they'd forgotten how precious real, uninterrupted time together could be.

Emma looked down, feeling a little sad. "I miss just being together without needing magic to make it feel special. I miss the way things were before we started using the clock all the time."

Max nodded, adding quietly, "Me too. I think the clock was supposed to be a reminder to appreciate time, not something to change it."

Mr. Baxter reached across the table, giving their hands a comforting squeeze. "That's a really wise way to look at it, both of you. The clock was a gift to help us remember how precious our time together is, not a tool to rely on for every little thing."

Mrs. Baxter looked around the table, her expression soft but determined. "Maybe... maybe we should leave the clock with Mr. Tockman a little while longer. I think it would do us good to spend more time without it, to learn to appreciate our time together as it is."

Emma and Max looked up, surprised but understanding. They had grown used to the idea of the clock being with them, but now they realized that its absence was teaching them an important lesson. The quiet, unhurried moments they'd shared in the past week had been a reminder of the simplicity and beauty of their everyday life—moments they might have missed if they'd had the clock.

"I think that's a good idea," Emma said, a small smile tugging at her lips. "We don't need magic to have a good time together. We just need each other."

Max nodded in agreement, feeling a sense of relief. "And when we do get the clock back someday, we'll know how to use it right. We'll use it only when it's really special, when we don't want to miss something important."

Mr. Baxter gave them an approving nod. "That sounds like a wonderful plan. The clock has taught us all an important lesson, and I think we'll be better for it. But let's take this time to reconnect without magic, to remember what it means to just be a family."

They finished their dinner slowly, savouring each other's company. The room was filled with laughter, stories, and warmth that needed no magic to feel special. And as they cleared the table and gathered in the living room for an evening of quiet games and conversation, they felt a deeper connection than they had in a long time.

The clock might have been sitting on Mr. Tockman's shelf, but the magic they felt was real—the kind of magic that came from simply being together, fully present, and appreciating each other's company.

Later that night, as Emma lay in bed, she reflected on the evening. She realized that she didn't miss the clock nearly as much as she'd thought she would. Instead, she felt a new appreciation for the family time they'd shared. She knew now that they didn't need a magical clock to make their moments meaningful; they simply needed to be together, to listen, and to laugh.

And somewhere, in his quiet shop, Mr. Tockman placed the clock gently on the shelf, smiling to himself. He knew that the Baxters had learned the lesson he'd hoped they would. The clock would be waiting for them when the time was right, but for now, it could rest, its magic untouched, while the Baxters discovered the joy of their real time together.

In the Baxter household, the family settled into a peaceful night, each of them filled with gratitude for the gift they already had—the gift of time, just as it was.

Part 5: Rediscovering Time
Chapter 21: A New Kind of Time

With the clock still resting at Tockman's Clocks, the Baxters began to find their own ways to slow down. At first, it felt strange not to have the magical assurance of extra time for special moments, but soon, they found that they didn't miss the clock as much as they'd thought. Instead, they began to appreciate the natural pace of their days, and each of them found joy in the smallest things.

One crisp Saturday morning, Mr. Baxter suggested an idea that would become a family favorite.

"Why don't we go for a walk?" he said, his voice bright with excitement. "We can explore the trails by the river, and maybe even bring some snacks for a picnic."

Emma and Max's faces lit up. They'd walked those trails before, but it had been a while, and the idea of a leisurely outing sounded perfect.

The family packed a small picnic, filled a thermos with hot chocolate, and bundled up in cozy jackets before setting out. As they walked along the winding path by the river, they breathed in the fresh, crisp air, taking in the golden autumn leaves and the gentle rustle of the wind. Each step felt unhurried, each moment savoured without needing the clock to stretch it out.

Emma noticed a squirrel scampering up a tree, pausing to watch it with a smile. Max found a smooth, flat stone and skipped it across the river, each bounce sending little ripples through the water. Mrs. Baxter spotted a patch of wildflowers, and they all took a moment to admire the colors and beauty of nature around them.

They spent the afternoon exploring the trails, finding new paths, and stopping to look at everything that caught their attention. They weren't in a hurry, and there was no need to rush. Each step, each laugh, each quiet moment filled them with a sense of peace that felt even richer than the clock's magic.

When they reached a sunny spot by the river, they laid out their picnic blanket and shared warm cups of hot chocolate, their breaths puffing out in little clouds of warmth as they laughed and told stories. Mr. Baxter taught them how to make leaf boats and float them on the water, each boat carrying little wishes they whispered into the autumn air.

That day became a treasured memory, not because they had used magic to stretch it out, but because they had been fully present, letting the day unfold at its own pace.

As the weeks went by, the Baxters began to create other routines that allowed them to savour time together. They started a new tradition of Friday family nights, where they'd gather in the living room for games, snacks, and stories. They played card games, told jokes, and even tried a puzzle or two, laughing as they struggled to find the last few pieces.

One Friday, as they sat around a board game, Emma looked up with a smile, her eyes sparkling. "This is even better than the clock's magic," she said. "It feels like we're creating our own way to make time special."

Mrs. Baxter nodded, her heart full. "It's because we're choosing to be together, to make each moment count without needing anything extra. Just us, as a family."

Max looked around at his family, his heart swelling with happiness. "I think we've found our own kind of magic. It's like... like we're learning how to slow down by ourselves."

On quiet Sunday mornings, Mr. Baxter would make pancakes, and the family would gather around the breakfast table, sharing plans and dreams. On weekday evenings, they'd sometimes take a short walk around the neighbourhood, pointing out the stars as they emerged in the evening sky. Without the clock, they had created a rhythm of small, meaningful moments that brought them closer together than ever before.

One evening, as Emma and Max sat with their parents around the living room, sharing hot tea and talking about their favorite memories, Mr. Baxter leaned back with a warm smile. "You know, I think the clock taught us something important."

Emma and Max looked up, curious.

"It taught us to appreciate what we already have," Mr. Baxter continued. "When we relied on it to make moments last, we were missing out on the beauty of each moment as it naturally unfolded. But now, we've learned to create special times together, just by being present."

Mrs. Baxter squeezed his hand, nodding. "And I think that's the most valuable lesson of all—that we don't need magic to feel connected or to make things special. We just need each other."

Emma thought about the past few weeks—the family walks, the game nights, the little conversations around the dinner table. She realized that each of these moments had felt just as magical as the times they'd used the clock, but in a different way. These moments didn't need to be extended or stretched out; they were perfect just as they were.

"Maybe when we get the clock back, we'll only use it on the rarest occasions," Max said thoughtfully. "Because I think we've found something better—real time together, just us."

They all agreed, feeling a deep sense of gratitude for the new pace of their lives. They had found a way to make each moment count, not by bending time to their will, but by letting time flow naturally and embracing each second with full hearts.

That night, as they went to bed, they each carried a quiet joy with them. They knew now that time, when appreciated for what it was, had a magic all its own. They had discovered a new kind of time—one they could create together, one that didn't need magic to be meaningful.

The clock would be waiting for them when they were ready, but for now, they felt perfectly content with the life they were building, one unhurried moment at a time.

Chapter 22: Mom and Dad's Special Moments

It was a cozy evening, and the Baxter family had gathered in the living room, each of them settled into their favorite spots with cups of tea and cocoa. The soft glow from the lamps bathed the room in warmth, creating the perfect atmosphere for quiet conversation and stories. With the clock still at Mr. Tockman's shop, they'd spent more time sharing these kinds of moments, discovering new ways to slow down and connect.

As they sipped their drinks, Emma looked up at her parents, her curiosity piqued. "Mom, Dad... do you have any special memories from when you were kids? Like, moments you remember really well, even though they happened a long time ago?"

Mrs. Baxter smiled, her eyes brightening at the thought. "Oh, I have so many! Little things, really, but they're the kind of memories that have stayed with me over the years."

Mr. Baxter nodded, chuckling softly. "It's funny how the simplest moments can end up meaning so much. Sometimes, you don't realize it until years later."

Emma and Max exchanged a glance, eager to hear more. They had always loved hearing about their parents' lives when they were young, but they'd never thought to ask about the moments that had truly stayed with them.

"Can you tell us a story?" Max asked, leaning forward with anticipation.

Mrs. Baxter set her tea down, her gaze drifting to the window, as if looking back in time. "Alright, here's one of my favourites. I remember one summer when I was about your age, Emma. My family didn't have much money, but every so often, my dad would surprise us with a treat.

One warm afternoon, he came home with a big bag of popsicles—every flavour you could imagine."

Emma's eyes widened. "What did you do?"

Mrs. Baxter laughed softly, her voice filled with fondness. "Well, we went outside and sat on the porch together. We didn't have air conditioning, so that cool treat felt like magic. I remember the way the sun was setting, how it turned everything a soft golden color, and how we all sat together, each of us picking our favorite flavour. It was just a simple evening, sitting on that porch, but I remember feeling so happy, so at peace."

Max looked thoughtful. "That sounds amazing. It's funny that something so small could mean so much."

Mrs. Baxter nodded, her expression warm. "That's the thing about time. It's not always the big moments or the grand adventures that stick with you. Sometimes, it's the smallest things—the sound of your dad laughing, the taste of that popsicle, the way the world looked as the sun set. Those little moments can carry a kind of magic all their own."

Mr. Baxter smiled, leaning forward as if ready to share his own memory. "Alright, here's one from when I was a bit older than you two. My family used to take weekend trips to a little lake nearby. We'd pack up the car with sandwiches, a cooler of lemonade, and an old radio that barely worked."

Emma grinned, imagining her dad as a boy. "What did you do at the lake?"

Mr. Baxter chuckled. "Mostly, we just sat by the water. My parents would relax in the shade, reading or talking, and my brother and I would fish. We weren't very good at it, but we'd sit there for hours with our lines in the water, laughing and daring each other to catch something big."

He paused, his eyes growing softer. "I remember one day in particular. It was cloudy, and the lake was so still it looked like glass. My brother and I caught a few tiny fish and threw them back, but mostly, we just sat there in the quiet, feeling like we had all the time in the world. I didn't realize it then, but those hours we spent by the lake, just talking and laughing, would become some of my most treasured memories."

Max nodded, captivated. "I think I get it. It wasn't really about the fish. It was about just being there, spending time together."

Mr. Baxter smiled proudly. "Exactly, Max. Those moments weren't planned, and they didn't need to be long or fancy. They were perfect because we were just there, fully present, without anything to rush off to or worry about. Sometimes, just being with the people you love, in a place that feels right, is more magical than anything."

Emma looked down at her cocoa, letting her parents' words settle in. She thought about all the little moments she'd already shared with her own family—the cozy mornings, the walks, the Friday game nights. Each of them was unique, and each felt special, just because they had all been there together.

Mrs. Baxter reached over, gently squeezing Emma's hand. "You know, magic isn't always about adding more time or making things last longer. Sometimes, it's about the way you feel in the moment. When you truly appreciate what's happening, it's like time slows down on its own."

Max glanced at his dad. "So, the clock is really just a reminder, isn't it? A way to help us see how precious each moment is."

Mr. Baxter nodded. "That's exactly right, Max. Life is made up of a million small moments, and the more we learn to appreciate each one, the more magical life feels. We don't need a clock to give us extra time—we just need to pay attention to the time we already have."

They sat in a comfortable silence for a while, each of them wrapped in their own thoughts. Emma and Max could almost picture their mom sitting on that porch, tasting a cold popsicle on a hot summer day, and their dad by the lake with his brother, surrounded by the quiet beauty of nature.

Emma spoke up, her voice soft. "I think maybe we've been looking at time the wrong way. Instead of trying to hold onto it, we just need to be in it, to let each moment feel special."

Mrs. Baxter smiled, giving her a gentle nod. "That's the secret, Emma. Time is precious because it keeps moving. Each moment is here for an instant, and then it's gone, but the memory of it stays with you."

Max glanced at the empty space on the shelf where the clock usually sat. He felt a deep respect for it, knowing now that its purpose wasn't to give them more time, but to remind them to treasure the time they had.

"I think when we get the clock back, we'll be ready to use it in the right way," he said thoughtfully. "We'll know that it's only for the rarest, most important moments—the ones we don't want to let slip by."

Mr. Baxter smiled, pride shining in his eyes. "I think you're right, Max. And until then, we'll keep finding ways to make time special, just by being together."

The family spent the rest of the evening sharing stories, laughing, and savouring each other's company. There was no magic clock to slow down the night, but they didn't need it. They'd discovered the true magic of time: that it didn't have to be extended to be meaningful—it simply had to be cherished.

As they all said goodnight and headed to bed, Emma and Max felt a quiet contentment, knowing that they were learning to appreciate time in a way that made every moment feel rich and full. They had come to understand that time, when spent with those you love, held a magic far greater than anything the clock could give.

And as the house grew still, the memories of their parents' stories lingered like a gentle glow, showing them that the simplest, most unplanned moments could be the most precious of all.

Chapter 23: Kids' Magic Hour

After their family meeting and hearing their parents' stories, Emma and Max felt inspired to find new ways to savour time without relying on the clock. They'd learned so much about how to appreciate moments as they naturally unfolded, but they still felt a pull to create something uniquely theirs—something to remind them of the importance of being present with each other.

One afternoon, as they walked home from school together, Emma turned to Max with an idea.

"What if we made our own special time?" she suggested. "A time every day when we can just... be together, without any distractions or interruptions."

Max's eyes lit up. "Like a magic hour! Just for us. We could do something fun or just talk, as long as it's something we both enjoy. And no phones, no rushing around—just us."

Emma grinned, loving the idea. "Exactly. We could make it a time where we're totally in the moment, like the way Mom and Dad talked about their memories."

They decided to call it their "magic hour" and agreed to set aside time each evening before dinner to be fully present with each other. It didn't need to be a full hour—sometimes it was just thirty minutes—but they promised each other that during that time, they'd put away all distractions and focus on making memories together, as siblings and friends.

That first evening, they chose to spend their magic hour in the backyard. The air was cool with the early evening breeze, and the sky was beginning to turn pink and gold as the sun dipped lower. They brought out a few blankets and sat side by side, looking up at the clouds.

"Look at that one," Emma pointed, giggling. "It looks like a giant bunny with floppy ears!"

Max squinted, following her gaze. "You're right! And that one looks like... a dragon. Or maybe a dog? I can't decide."

They spent the time lying back, pointing out different shapes in the clouds, making up stories about the "cloud creatures" they spotted. Emma decided that the "bunny cloud" was hopping to a magical forest, while Max insisted that his "dragon cloud" was guarding a hidden treasure in the sky. They laughed and joked, letting their imaginations run wild as the colors deepened in the sky above them.

When their magic hour was up, they both felt a sense of calm and happiness that they hadn't expected. It was different from the kind of fun they usually had; it felt deeper, like they'd shared something special that would stay with them.

The next evening, they chose to spend their magic hour in the living room, where they built a fort out of blankets and pillows. They each brought a flashlight and a favorite book, and as they read together, they took turns sharing funny lines or interesting facts. They didn't feel the need to hurry or rush through the time; they simply enjoyed being in each other's company, wrapped in the warmth of their cozy fort.

Over the next few weeks, their magic hour became a treasured part of each day. Sometimes they went outside to look at the stars, trying to spot constellations and making up their own stories about the night sky. Other times, they created drawings together, played a quick game, or simply talked about their day, sharing their highs and lows and things that made them laugh.

One evening, as they sat at the kitchen table during their magic hour, each of them working on their own little drawing, Emma looked up at Max, her eyes filled with warmth.

"I think this is the best part of my day," she said quietly. "Our magic hour, I mean. It feels... special. Like we're really taking the time to know each other."

Max nodded, feeling the same way. "Me too. And I think what makes it magic is that we're just being here, not thinking about anything else."

They both realized that the time they spent together during their magic hour was teaching them how to be present in a way that didn't need any magical clock. They had discovered that when they focused on each other, without distractions or rushing, each moment felt richer and more meaningful.

One Friday evening, their parents noticed them setting up their magic hour in the living room and came over, curious.

"What are you two up to?" Mrs. Baxter asked, smiling as she watched them set up a board game.

Emma looked up, smiling back. "We've started something we call 'magic hour.' Every day, we spend a little time together without phones or homework or anything. We just focus on being together."

Mr. Baxter's eyes twinkled with pride. "That sounds wonderful. I think you two have discovered something very important. Real magic doesn't need anything extra—it's about being fully present, appreciating the people around you."

Mrs. Baxter gave them each a hug. "I'm so proud of you both. You've found a way to create your own special time, and I think that's more magical than any clock could be."

As the weeks went by, Emma and Max continued their magic hour, finding new ways to enjoy each other's company. They baked cookies, tried to teach each other little skills like drawing animals or making paper airplanes, and sometimes even worked on puzzles. Each moment felt like a tiny memory they were building together, one that didn't need any stretching or magic to be meaningful.

Through their magic hour, they had come to understand the true gift of time—how even the simplest activities could feel special if they approached them with care and attention.

One evening, as they finished their magic hour and headed to the dinner table, Max looked over at Emma, a quiet smile on his face.

"You know, I think we've found our own kind of magic," he said thoughtfully. "And it's something we'll always have, even without the clock."

Emma nodded, feeling a warmth in her heart. "Yeah, we'll have these memories forever. And I think… I think that's what makes time so special. It's not about making it last longer—it's about making it count."

As they joined their parents for dinner, they each felt a deep sense of gratitude for the journey they had taken with the clock. They had learned to appreciate every moment and to savour their time together in a way that made each day feel fuller and more meaningful.

Their magic hour became a cherished tradition, one they looked forward to each day, knowing that no matter how busy or rushed life became, they would always have that little space of time set aside just for each other.

And as the sun set outside, casting a soft glow over the house, Emma and Max knew that they had discovered a magic far greater than any clock could offer—the magic of being present, of truly seeing each other, and of creating memories that would last a lifetime.

Chapter 24: The Treasure Hunt

One rainy Saturday afternoon, the Baxters found themselves stuck indoors. The rain drummed steadily against the windows, casting a soft, cozy light throughout the house, but after a morning of board games, books, and hot chocolate, they were all starting to feel a bit restless.

"Why don't we come up with something new to do together?" Mr. Baxter suggested, looking around the room with a smile. "Something that lets us be creative and have a bit of fun."

Emma's eyes lit up. "What if we made a game? Like a treasure hunt around the house?"

Max grinned, instantly on board. "Yes! We could each take turns hiding little 'treasures' and then leave clues for everyone else to find them!"

Mrs. Baxter nodded, clearly excited by the idea. "I love it! We can use things we already have around the house as treasures, and everyone can take turns hiding and searching. We'll make it a real adventure."

With that, the family sprang into action, each of them gathering small, meaningful objects to hide around the house. Emma picked a tiny silver keychain shaped like a heart, a gift from her grandmother. Max chose a smooth, colorful marble he'd kept since he was little, and Mr. and Mrs. Baxter each found their own special treasures—a seashell from a family beach trip and a tiny old coin Mr. Baxter had saved from a trip abroad.

After setting a few ground rules, they started the game, with Emma going first. She carefully hid her heart-shaped keychain in a little nook by the bookshelves and then scribbled a clue on a small slip of paper: "Where the stories sit and dreams begin, the heart of the treasure hides within."

Emma handed the clue to her family, grinning with excitement as they tried to figure it out. Max read it aloud, his brow furrowing in thought. "Hmm... 'where the stories sit'... it has to be the bookshelves!"

They all hurried over to the bookshelves, eagerly searching each nook and cranny until Mrs. Baxter let out a little cry of delight. "Here it is!" she said, holding up the tiny heart keychain.

They cheered, and Emma beamed with pride. The game was off to a perfect start, and each clue brought new laughter and excitement. For each treasure, they created clever clues and hid the items in the most unexpected spots. Max's marble was hidden in an old flower pot, Mrs. Baxter's seashell was tucked inside a tea tin, and Mr. Baxter's coin was placed under the couch cushions.

Each time they found a treasure, they laughed and celebrated as if they'd uncovered a rare prize. They took turns running around the house, piecing together clues, and enjoying the thrill of each discovery.

After a few rounds, they decided to add a twist to the game. Instead of hiding personal items, they each created small "treasure notes"—little messages or drawings that would become keepsakes of the day. Emma sketched a little picture of the family at the beach, with the words, "My treasure is spending time with you." Max wrote a joke on his, wanting to bring a smile to everyone's face, and Mr. and Mrs. Baxter each wrote small, heartfelt notes that reminded the family of shared memories.

With this new twist, the treasure hunt took on an even more meaningful layer. They found themselves not only searching for hidden objects but for little reminders of their love and connection as a family. The game became a mixture of laughter and warm, quiet moments as they read each message and remembered why these times together were so precious.

When they found Emma's drawing tucked inside her father's old hat, they all gathered around to look at it, admiring the way she'd captured a moment they all treasured.

"This is perfect, Emma," Mrs. Baxter said, giving her daughter a hug. "These little memories are the best kind of treasure."

Max grinned as he held up his note, a joke that had everyone laughing until their sides hurt: "What kind of treasure hides in a house? One that's not lost, just waiting to be found!"

They all giggled, and Mr. Baxter clapped him on the shoulder. "You're right, Max. And I think that's exactly what we've been doing—finding treasures that were here all along."

The final note they found was from Mrs. Baxter, hidden under a cushion in her favorite armchair. It simply read, "Time spent together is the best treasure of all." They read it in silence, each of them feeling the truth of those words.

As the day went on, they continued to hide and find treasures, each new discovery bringing fresh laughter and a sense of togetherness. By evening, the house was filled with little notes and keepsakes from the day's game, each a reminder of the special time they'd spent together.

When they finally gathered in the living room for dinner, they sat surrounded by their "treasures," smiling as they looked at each little note, drawing, and keepsake they'd uncovered. The treasure hunt had reminded them that the greatest joys didn't come from the things they found, but from the time they'd spent searching and laughing together.

Mr. Baxter raised his glass, his face filled with warmth. "To the best kind of treasure—time spent together."

They all raised their glasses, clinking them with a cheer. "To time together!"

That night, as they got ready for bed, Emma and Max felt a sense of happiness and peace that didn't come from any magical clock, but from the simple joy of being with each other, of creating memories that would stay with them forever. They had discovered that treasure wasn't about material things, but about moments shared and memories made.

The treasure hunt became a new family tradition. Every so often, one of them would start a new round, hiding little notes or small objects for the others to find, each "treasure" filled with love, humour, or a memory. And as they played, they were reminded that the best treasures were not things they could hold, but moments they could feel—moments they would carry with them long after the game was over.

In the quiet of the evening, as they drifted off to sleep, Emma and Max felt a deep gratitude for their family, for the time they shared, and for the simple joy of being together. They knew that these moments were the true treasures, and they were grateful for everyone.

Chapter 25: Making Time for Friends

After weeks of practicing being more present with their family, Emma and Max began noticing a new feeling that made their days seem a bit fuller, richer. They no longer needed the magical clock to create special moments with their family; they had discovered that being present, mindful, and grateful allowed them to enjoy each second.

One sunny afternoon, Emma and Max invited their friends, Leo and Mia, over to play in the backyard. They'd planned a day full of fun games: soccer, tag, and even a scavenger hunt that the two of them had put together. But as their friends arrived, both Emma and Max felt a twinge of worry.

"It always feels like these days go by so fast," Emma whispered to Max as they watched Leo and Mia run up to the yard. "It's like we blink, and it's time for everyone to go home."

Max nodded, sharing her thoughts. "Yeah, I wish we could make the day last a little longer, like we do with family time. But we don't have the clock, and besides, it's only for family moments."

Emma's face brightened as she had an idea. "What if we tried to make the time slow down on our own? Mr. Tockman always said that magic was about being present, really paying attention. Maybe if we focus, we can 'stretch' time in our minds."

Max thought about it, realizing that it might just work. After all, they'd been practicing being more present, and it had made their moments with family feel more special. Why not try it with friends, too?

They joined Leo and Mia in the yard, and instead of jumping right into their games, they took a moment to look around, breathing in the fresh air and appreciating the feeling of the warm sunlight on their faces.

"Let's start with a scavenger hunt," Max suggested, handing each of them a list of things to find: a red leaf, a small rock shaped like a triangle, a yellow flower, and something that reminded them of a happy memory.

Leo and Mia grinned, excitement in their eyes, and they set off around the yard, laughing and searching. Emma and Max focused on each step, paying close attention to the colors of the leaves, the texture of the rocks, and the gentle rustle of the trees in the breeze. Each moment felt full, as if they were noticing every little detail, savouring the thrill of the hunt.

As they searched, Mia found a small yellow flower and held it up with a bright smile. "This one reminds me of my grandma's garden! She used to plant these every spring."

Leo picked up a smooth rock, turning it over in his hands. "Look, it's almost shaped like a heart," he said, proudly showing it to everyone. "I'm keeping this one as a souvenir."

Instead of rushing to find everything on their lists, they took time to appreciate each "treasure" they uncovered, sharing stories and laughing together. They moved on to a game of soccer, but even then, Emma and Max practiced being fully present, enjoying every laugh, every sprint, every kick.

Max noticed that time seemed to slow down, almost like it did when they used the clock, even though they hadn't used magic at all. Each laugh, each cheer, each shared glance felt richer, as though the world had expanded to hold every moment.

After a while, the four of them flopped down on the grass, breathing heavily and staring up at the sky. Clouds drifted lazily by, and the world felt quiet and peaceful.

Leo looked over at them, smiling. "This is the best day ever. I don't even feel like we need to rush into the next game or anything."

Emma grinned, her heart warm. "Yeah. Sometimes, just paying attention to what's happening right now makes everything feel... fuller."

Mia nodded in agreement, looking thoughtful. "It's like we don't need to do a hundred things to make the day feel special. Just being here, enjoying each other's company, makes it amazing."

Max looked up at the sky, feeling a deep sense of contentment. He realized that the magic of slowing down time wasn't limited to family or the clock. By being present, by truly appreciating each moment with their friends, they could make time feel more meaningful.

They spent the rest of the day in this peaceful rhythm, moving from one game to the next but never feeling the need to hurry. They paused to share stories, pointed out little things they noticed, and let each moment stretch out naturally, allowing them to feel fully connected with each other.

As the afternoon wore on and the sun began to set, they all gathered on the porch with cups of lemonade, savouring the quiet moments and watching the sky turn shades of pink and orange.

Leo looked over at Emma and Max, smiling. "I don't know what it is, but today felt different. It was like... like we weren't just playing, but really enjoying each minute."

Max smiled, exchanging a knowing glance with Emma. "Yeah, we realized that when you pay attention to each moment, it feels like time slows down on its own."

Mia nodded, looking thoughtful. "I'm going to remember this. We don't always need to be doing something big to make a day special. Sometimes, just being together and paying attention is enough."

As their friends left that evening, Emma and Max felt a deep sense of satisfaction. They'd learned that the magic of slowing down time could be found in the way they chose to approach each moment. With friends, just as with family, they could create memories that felt rich and lasting, all by simply being present.

At dinner that night, they told their parents about their day and shared what they'd learned. Mr. Baxter smiled, nodding in understanding.

"You two have discovered something important. Time doesn't need magic to be meaningful. When you're fully present, appreciating each moment, you create your own magic."

Mrs. Baxter reached across the table, holding each of their hands. "You've found a gift that you can carry with you wherever you go. Being present is the best way to make each day special, no matter who you're with."

Emma and Max nodded, feeling grateful for the lesson they had learned with their friends. They knew now that the magic of time wasn't about slowing or stretching it—it was about savouring it, paying attention, and appreciating the people they were with.

And as they went to bed that night, they felt a quiet peace, knowing that they didn't need a magical clock to make time meaningful. They could create magic in every moment, whether with family, friends, or even on their own, by simply being present and treasuring the time they had.

Chapter 26: A Picnic Day

One Saturday morning, the Baxter family woke up to a perfect spring day. The sky was clear and blue, and the sun cast a warm, inviting glow over everything. Mrs. Baxter, feeling the excitement of a rare beautiful weekend, had an idea.

"Why don't we have a picnic today?" she suggested at breakfast, her face lighting up. "We can pack some sandwiches, a few treats, and just spend the whole day outside together."

Emma and Max immediately perked up at the idea. They loved being outdoors, and a picnic meant a whole day of adventure without any schedules or to-do lists. Mr. Baxter grinned, nodding his approval.

"I'll bring the old picnic blanket," he said, already heading to the closet. "And let's keep it simple—no phones, no clocks, nothing to distract us. Just a day to enjoy each other's company."

With that, they all pitched in to prepare the picnic. Emma helped Mrs. Baxter make sandwiches with turkey, cheese, and crisp lettuce, while Max filled a basket with fruit, chips, and chocolate chip cookies they'd baked the night before. They added a thermos of lemonade, a few napkins, and a deck of cards for games.

Within an hour, they were ready to go, and they set off for the nearby park. It was a spot they'd visited before, with big trees and plenty of grassy areas perfect for spreading out a picnic blanket. As they arrived, they found a spot under a tall, leafy tree and laid out the blanket, feeling the cool grass beneath their feet.

They took a few minutes to settle in, unpacking the food and stretching out in the warm sunshine. Birds chirped overhead, and the light breeze carried the fresh scent of blooming flowers.

Emma sighed happily, looking around. "This is perfect. It's like we have the whole world to ourselves."

Max nodded, closing his eyes as he lay back on the blanket. "Yeah, I could stay here all day."

And so, they did. The day unfolded slowly, peacefully, with no rush and no distractions. They took their time eating, savouring each bite of their sandwiches, enjoying the sweetness of the lemonade, and laughing as crumbs scattered onto the blanket. For the first time in a while, they didn't feel any need to check the time or wonder what was next. They were fully present, focused only on each other.

After lunch, they played a few rounds of cards. Max and Emma were fiercely competitive, trying to outdo each other in every game, while their parents laughed and joined in. They swapped stories from school and work, shared their favorite jokes, and made silly bets about who would win the next game.

As the afternoon wore on, they decided to explore a little, wandering through the park together. They spotted flowers blooming in vivid colors, found a tiny stream where they skipped stones, and even lay in the grass to watch the clouds drift by. Each moment felt like a small adventure, something special to remember.

Emma looked over at her parents, smiling. "It feels like time is going slower today. Like we're making every minute count."

Mrs. Baxter nodded, holding her daughter's hand as they walked along a path dappled with sunlight. "That's the beauty of focusing on each other, sweetheart. When we pay attention to each other instead of the time, it feels like we have all the time in the world."

Max caught up to them, skipping a smooth stone he'd found in the stream. "I don't even feel like checking a clock," he admitted. "I think… I think I like not knowing what time it is. It's like we're free to just be here, without worrying about when it ends."

Mr. Baxter smiled, ruffling Max's hair. "Exactly. It's amazing how natural time feels when we're not trying to control it, isn't it? Sometimes, just letting go and enjoying each moment as it comes is the best way to make memories."

They returned to the picnic blanket, lying back and gazing up at the sky as it slowly shifted from bright blue to a soft, golden hue.

They shared stories about their favorite family moments, laughed at old memories, and dreamed up new adventures they wanted to go on someday.

Eventually, as the sun began to dip lower, casting a warm, amber glow over the park, they unpacked the cookies and enjoyed dessert together, each bite filled with the sweetness of the day. The laughter and conversation drifted along with the breeze, carrying with it the happiness of a day well spent.

As they packed up to head home, Emma took one last look at the park, feeling a deep sense of peace. "I think this is one of my favorite days ever," she said softly.

Max nodded, grinning. "Me too. And we didn't even need magic to make it feel special. Just being here together made it perfect."

Mrs. Baxter put her arms around both of them, her eyes filled with warmth. "That's because time is most beautiful when we share it with the people we love. We didn't need a clock to make today last—we just needed each other."

As they walked home together, Emma and Max felt the calm of the day settle in their hearts. They realized that they didn't need to stretch or control time to make it feel magical. When they focused on each other, on their laughter, and on the little moments, each second felt as though it contained all the joy they could ever need.

Later that evening, as they unpacked the picnic basket and settled into the comfort of home, they shared stories of the day with quiet smiles. It had been a simple day, but one that reminded them of the real magic in their lives—the people around them, the love they shared, and the memories they made together.

And as they drifted off to sleep, each of them felt a quiet gratitude, knowing that true magic wasn't in the stretching or slowing of time but in savouring it, exactly as it was.

Part 6: The Final Secret of the Clock
Chapter 27: A Surprise from Mr. Tockman

After weeks of enjoying time together without the magical clock, the Baxters decided it was time to visit Tockman's Clocks. They missed the little timepiece and looked forward to seeing Mr. Tockman again, ready to share the lessons they'd learned about savouring moments and creating memories on their own.

On a sunny Saturday morning, they set off for Mr. Tockman's shop. As they walked through the familiar cobbled streets, Emma and Max chatted excitedly about what they would tell him. They were proud of how far they'd come and eager to show Mr. Tockman that they understood the true value of the clock's magic.

When they arrived at the little shop, the golden sign swung gently in the breeze, the delicate lettering catching the morning light: Tockman's Clocks: Timepieces and Wonders. Emma and Max exchanged a glance, feeling a thrill of anticipation as they pushed open the door.

But instead of the usual soft chime and the warm sight of Mr. Tockman behind his counter, the shop felt different. The clocks on the walls ticked softly, as always, filling the room with their comforting rhythm, but the familiar figure of Mr. Tockman was nowhere to be seen. Instead, a single note lay on the counter, carefully folded and sealed with a small, golden stamp shaped like a clock.

Mr. Baxter picked up the note, his brow furrowing in curiosity. "It looks like Mr. Tockman isn't here," he murmured, turning the note over in his hands. "But he left us something."

Emma and Max leaned closer, their eyes widening as they watched their father open the note. Inside was a simple message, written in Mr. Tockman's familiar, elegant handwriting.

Dear Baxter Family,

I had a feeling you'd be visiting today, and while I'm not here in person, I wanted to leave you with a message and a little surprise. I can see that your time away from the clock has been full of the magic I hoped you'd find on your own. You've discovered that the greatest treasures are often those we create in the present moment, without needing to stretch or change time.

But there's one last gift I'd like to share with you. You'll find it waiting in a place where memories rest, where laughter and joy have gathered. Look to your own home to uncover this final gift. It's something I hope will remind you of the lessons you've learned and the journey you've taken as a family.

With warmest regards,
Mr. Tockman

P.S. Don't worry about the clock here—it will remain safe with me, ready whenever you feel it is truly needed.

The Baxters exchanged surprised glances, each of them feeling a mix of curiosity and wonder. A gift in their home? What could it be, and how would they find it?

Emma clutched the note, her heart racing with excitement. "He left us a gift, but he didn't say what it was. It could be anything!"

Max's eyes sparkled as he thought over the words. "He said to look in a place where memories rest. Do you think he means a specific room in our house?"

Mrs. Baxter nodded thoughtfully. "It sounds like it. Mr. Tockman knows how special certain places in our home are to us. Maybe it's somewhere we've spent a lot of time together."

They all considered the possibilities as they walked home, talking excitedly about where Mr. Tockman's final gift might be hidden. Each of them had different ideas—the living room, where they shared family nights and cozy chats, or maybe the backyard, where they'd had countless outdoor adventures together. Wherever it was, they knew it would be a place that held memories they treasured.

When they arrived back home, they began their search, each of them moving quietly through the rooms, looking for any clue that might reveal Mr. Tockman's gift. They checked the familiar spots where they'd shared moments of joy—the kitchen, with its delicious smells and laughter, the living room, where they'd spent so many evenings together, and even the backyard, which had been the setting for countless family games and picnics.

But after a careful search, they still hadn't found anything unusual. Just as they were about to gather in the living room to discuss their next idea, Emma suddenly remembered something.

"The old trunk!" she exclaimed, her eyes lighting up. "In the attic! We keep all kinds of family things in there—old photos, keepsakes, things from when Max and I were little."

Max's face lit up as he realized she might be right. "Of course! If there's any place where memories rest, it's in that trunk."

With renewed excitement, they all headed up to the attic. The room was filled with the soft scent of cedar and a warm, familiar coziness. In the corner, beneath a slant of sunlight from the attic window, sat the old wooden trunk. It was a place they rarely visited, but each time they opened it, it felt like stepping into a little piece of family history.

Mr. Baxter carefully opened the trunk, lifting the lid with a reverence reserved for precious things. Inside were stacks of photo albums, little boxes filled with trinkets, and the kind of keepsakes that carried years of memories. And there, resting on top of a soft blue blanket, was a small, neatly wrapped package tied with a simple ribbon.

Emma gasped, reaching for it with gentle hands. She held it up, looking at her family with wide eyes. "This must be it. Mr. Tockman's gift."

The package felt light but firm, and the wrapping paper was decorated with tiny, hand-drawn clocks. Emma handed it to her father, who untied the ribbon carefully, each of them holding their breath in anticipation.

But when they unwrapped the paper, they found only another note, folded neatly with Mr. Tockman's handwriting on the front: Open this together, when the moment feels right.

They looked at each other, each of them feeling a rush of wonder. Mr. Tockman had left them a mystery, something meant for a special moment. It wasn't just an ordinary gift; it was something that would wait until they felt it was truly needed, something to be revealed when the time was right.

Mrs. Baxter smiled, holding the note as though it were a precious treasure. "I think Mr. Tockman wants us to decide when the right moment is, just like with the clock."

Mr. Baxter nodded. "It's like he's reminding us that the true magic of any gift lies in when we choose to use it. For now, let's keep this safely in the trunk, so it'll be waiting for us when the time is right."

Emma and Max both nodded, feeling the sense of excitement that came with knowing a secret was waiting for them. They didn't need to rush to find out what was inside; they'd learned that the most special moments often came when they were least expected, unfolding naturally and without hurry.

They carefully placed the note back in the trunk, closing the lid and leaving Mr. Tockman's final gift safely tucked away. As they went back downstairs, they each felt a quiet sense of happiness, knowing that when the right moment arrived, they would have something special to share together.

And in that quiet attic, the gift would wait, holding within it a promise of one more adventure, one that would come when they were ready to embrace it with full hearts and open minds.

Chapter 28: The Clock's Final Gift

Weeks had passed since their trip to the attic, and life had settled into its natural, unhurried rhythm. The Baxters continued to cherish the small, everyday moments that made their family life so full, carrying forward everything they'd learned about the magic of time. The mysterious note from Mr. Tockman stayed safely tucked away in the old trunk, waiting for the moment that felt right.

One evening, as they gathered in the living room for a quiet night together, Mrs. Baxter brought up the note.

"I think tonight might be the right moment," she said, her eyes filled with warmth as she looked around at her family. "We've spent all this time learning about the importance of being present, of savouring our moments together. Maybe it's time we find out what Mr. Tockman's final gift is."

Emma and Max nodded eagerly, each of them filled with a gentle excitement. Mr. Baxter retrieved the note from the trunk, and they gathered close together as he unfolded it, each of them leaning in to see Mr. Tockman's familiar handwriting.

The message was short, but it felt as though each word held a special weight.

Dear Baxter Family,

You have discovered what I had hoped for all along: the real magic of time doesn't live in a clock or in a spell—it lives in your hearts. The moments you've shared, the memories you've created, and the love you've shown each other have brought the magic of the clock into your lives in a way that will last forever.

The clock's purpose was to guide you toward this understanding, and now, you no longer need it to remind you of what's most precious. Its magic has become a part of you, helping you see the beauty in each second and the value of every day you share together.

THE CLOCKMAKER'S SECRET GIFT

So, my dear friends, the clock has given its final gift—to live in your hearts as a gentle reminder to cherish each moment, wherever life takes you. May you carry this magic with you always.

With all my best wishes,

Mr. Tockman

The family sat in silence for a moment, letting the words settle over them. Emma felt her eyes well up, understanding the true beauty of Mr. Tockman's message. The clock had been a guide, yes, but it had always been leading them back to something much closer—something they'd already had in their hearts all along.

Max looked around at his family, a soft smile forming on his face. "The magic was never really about slowing down time, was it? It was about helping us see how much we already have."

Mrs. Baxter squeezed his hand, her face filled with love and understanding. "Exactly, Max. We thought we needed the clock to make moments last, but we've learned that when we're truly present, each moment feels full and beautiful just as it is."

Mr. Baxter nodded, a quiet pride in his eyes. "Mr. Tockman's gift was teaching us how to carry that magic forward. Now, we know that every moment we spend together is something to be treasured, even without a clock to guide us."

Emma looked at her family, her heart filled with gratitude. "The clock's magic is inside us now. It's like we've learned how to see time differently, to feel it in our hearts instead of trying to control it."

They all shared a warm, contented silence, each of them feeling the truth of Mr. Tockman's words. The clock had been more than just an object—it had been a teacher, helping them uncover the real magic of time. They realized that the clock's purpose had always been to bring them to this understanding, to help them see that time was precious because of the love they shared and the memories they made together.

As the evening wore on, they shared stories, laughter, and quiet moments, each of them feeling the weight of time in a new, beautiful way. They knew that every day they spent together would now feel richer, guided by the gentle reminder that time was theirs to cherish, to appreciate, and to live fully.

When it was time for bed, they put Mr. Tockman's note back in the trunk, not as a secret to keep hidden, but as a treasured reminder of their journey. They understood now that the clock's magic was alive in them, a part of who they were as a family.

And as they drifted off to sleep that night, each of them felt the quiet, enduring gift that Mr. Tockman had given them—a gift that needed no clock, no extra time, only an open heart and a willingness to embrace each moment.

The clock's final gift had been one they would carry with them always: the knowledge that time is most beautiful when it's spent with those you love, and that each moment, no matter how small, is a treasure all its own.

Chapter 29: The Power Within

After reading Mr. Tockman's final note, the Baxters felt a renewed sense of peace and happiness. They'd learned that the magic of the clock was not in its ability to slow down time, but in the way it had taught them to value the moments they shared. They knew now that each of them held the power to make time feel special, to appreciate life simply by being present and grateful.

The next morning, as sunlight streamed through the windows and filled the house with warmth, Emma found herself thinking about how they could carry this lesson forward. She went to the kitchen, where she found her mom pouring coffee and her dad reading the morning paper. Max joined them, still rubbing the sleep from his eyes, and they all settled into a comfortable silence, savouring the start of a new day.

Emma looked around at her family, feeling that familiar warmth in her chest, the one she'd felt so many times over the past few weeks. It was as though the magic of the clock was still with them, woven into the air around them.

"Do you think," she began, glancing at her parents and then at Max, "that we have the power to slow down time on our own now? Like… just by being here together?"

Mrs. Baxter smiled, nodding thoughtfully. "Yes, Emma. I think that's exactly what Mr. Tockman was trying to show us. We don't need the clock to remind us to appreciate life anymore. We have that power within us."

Max looked at her, a smile spreading across his face. "So, it's like the magic is a part of us now. We can make each moment feel longer, just by paying attention and being grateful."

Mr. Baxter put down his newspaper, his eyes warm and full of pride. "Exactly, Max. It's as if the clock has taught us a skill that we can use forever—one that doesn't need any outside help. When we focus on each other, on the things that bring us joy, time naturally feels slower and richer."

They decided to put this newfound power to the test by planning a simple day together, focusing on creating memories without any distractions. They chose to spend the day in their backyard, enjoying the beauty of the outdoors, each other's company, and the quiet magic of being fully present.

After breakfast, they spread out blankets under the big oak tree and lay in the dappled sunlight, feeling the cool grass beneath them. They pointed out birds in the trees, shared stories about past adventures, and made up funny characters based on the shapes of the clouds. Each laugh, each gentle breeze, each quiet moment felt like it stretched, like time was slowing down to let them savour every second.

At one point, Max sat up, a thoughtful look on his face. "I think what makes time feel longer isn't just focusing on each other. It's also about letting go of everything else—like not worrying about what comes next or what we have to do later."

Emma nodded, lying back with her arms behind her head. "Yeah. It's like we're just here, in this exact moment, not anywhere else. That makes it feel special."

As they continued their day, they took turns sharing things they were grateful for, things they'd noticed about each other, and little moments they wanted to remember. They felt no rush, no need to check the time. In their hearts, they'd found the magic to slow down, to make each second feel like a treasure simply by appreciating it.

In the afternoon, they made sandwiches together, each of them contributing their favorite toppings and making the task a fun little adventure. They joked about the "perfect sandwich" and laughed at their creative combinations. Emma made a silly face with pickles and cheese, and Max created a "double-decker special" that barely fit in his mouth. The simple meal felt like a feast, and they savoured each bite, laughing and talking about nothing in particular but feeling completely connected.

As the day went on, Emma realized that the clock had given them something priceless: the understanding that time was most meaningful when they chose to truly experience it. They didn't need a special occasion or a magical object to make moments count—they only needed each other and the willingness to pay attention to the present.

In the golden light of the late afternoon, Mrs. Baxter looked around at her family, her heart full. "I think we've learned the greatest magic of all—that we're the ones who can make time feel beautiful. It's a choice we make, every day, by choosing to be here, fully present, with each other."

Mr. Baxter nodded, his voice soft. "Mr. Tockman gave us a gift that will last forever. He showed us that time doesn't need to be stretched or slowed. It just needs to be lived."

Emma smiled, glancing at Max, who grinned back. They understood now that this was the true power the clock had given them—not the ability to change time, but to cherish it as it was.

As the sun began to set and the day drew to a close, they stayed out in the yard, watching the sky turn shades of pink and orange. They didn't feel the usual pang of regret or wish for more time, because they knew that they had fully experienced each second. They felt a quiet satisfaction, knowing that they had truly lived their day to the fullest.

That evening, as they gathered in the living room to share one last story before bed, they felt the gentle presence of the clock's magic, woven into their hearts. They knew that they would carry this gift forward, always able to slow down and appreciate life, with or without a clock to remind them.

And as they said goodnight, each of them felt the same quiet joy, knowing that they held within them the power to make time special, to see life with grateful eyes, and to find magic in every moment they chose to cherish.

Chapter 30: Goodbye to the Shop

A few weeks had passed since the Baxters had read Mr. Tockman's final note, and life felt fuller and more meaningful than ever. They had spent each day appreciating their moments together, practicing the art of slowing down and savouring time without needing the clock's magic. They'd discovered the joy of truly living in the present, and every moment felt like a gift.

One Saturday morning, Emma and Max had an idea.

"Why don't we go see Mr. Tockman?" Emma suggested over breakfast, her face bright with excitement. "I want to thank him for everything he taught us. We couldn't have discovered all of this without him."

Max nodded eagerly. "Yes! We owe him so much, and I want him to know that we understand the real magic now. I think he'd like to know how much he's helped us."

Their parents agreed, feeling that a visit to Tockman's Clocks would be the perfect way to express their gratitude. After breakfast, they gathered as a family and set off through the familiar cobbled streets, looking forward to seeing Mr. Tockman and sharing everything they'd learned.

But as they approached the shop, something felt different. The usual soft glow from the windows was missing, and the golden sign above the door hung still and silent, with a faint layer of dust on it. When they reached the door, they saw a small, hand-written note taped to the glass.

To the Baxters and to all who have visited,

Thank you for sharing this journey of time and magic with me.

I've decided that it's time for me to move on, but the lessons we've shared will remain, both in this shop and in your hearts.

Remember that true magic is found in the way you live, in the time you spend with loved ones, and in the moments you choose to cherish.

With all my best wishes,
Mr. Tockman

The Baxters stared at the note, feeling a mixture of surprise and sadness. Mr. Tockman had closed his shop without saying goodbye, leaving only this gentle farewell in his place. Emma and Max felt their hearts sink slightly, realizing they wouldn't get to see the clockmaker again.

Mrs. Baxter placed a comforting hand on their shoulders. "It's hard to say goodbye, but I think Mr. Tockman knew this was part of the journey. He taught us everything he needed to, and he trusted us to carry his lessons forward."

Mr. Baxter nodded, his expression thoughtful. "He gave us the gift of time in a way that goes beyond his shop or even the clock itself. What matters now is how we carry that magic in our lives."

Emma and Max exchanged a quiet look, each of them understanding that Mr. Tockman's lessons were, in a way, his final gift. They had learned everything he'd hoped for them to discover—not only how to cherish their moments but how to find the magic in time, even without a clock to remind them.

They stood in front of the shop for a while, taking in the memories they'd shared there, from the first time they'd entered, drawn in by Mr. Tockman's warmth and wonder, to the lessons he'd shared with them, both big and small. Each moment in the shop had been a part of their journey, leading them to this moment where they could say goodbye with hearts full of gratitude.

Max took a deep breath, a small smile spreading across his face. "Mr. Tockman's right. The magic isn't really in the shop or even in the clock. It's in us now. We can carry it with us wherever we go."

Emma nodded, her voice soft but certain. "We'll never forget what he taught us. We'll keep making memories and savouring our time, just like he showed us."

Together, they each took a last look at the shop, imagining the way it had felt when Mr. Tockman had welcomed them inside, always eager to share his wisdom and his gentle reminders about the beauty of time. They knew they would carry these memories forward, woven into the moments they would create as a family.

And as they walked away, the Baxters felt a deep sense of peace, knowing that the shop and Mr. Tockman's legacy would live on in their hearts. They had found the power to make time meaningful on their own, and they would continue to cherish every day, holding close the magic of being present and truly valuing the people they loved.

As they walked back home, they talked about the memories they'd made in the shop and the lessons they would continue to practice. They knew now that time didn't need to be slowed down or extended to be beautiful—it simply needed to be embraced with open hearts.

From that day on, the Baxters lived each moment with a renewed sense of gratitude. Every laugh, every story, every shared meal felt like a treasure, a memory waiting to be made. They didn't need Mr. Tockman's shop or even the clock to remind them of the magic they held; it was within them, alive and present in the way they lived.

In their hearts, they carried the clockmaker's lessons, each one a reminder of the gift of time and the beauty of a life well-loved. And as they moved forward, they knew that the magic of time, once discovered, was theirs to hold forever.

Chapter 31: Happily Ever After, Slowed Down

With Mr. Tockman's shop closed and the clock left behind, the Baxters felt as though they had reached a new chapter in their lives. They carried with them everything the clockmaker had taught them, from the magic of being present to the art of savouring time. They no longer needed the clock to remind them to slow down; they had made it a part of who they were.

In the weeks and months that followed, they began to create their own family traditions, each one designed to help them focus on the beauty of the moment. Friday nights became their official family game night, where they'd gather in the living room to play cards, tell stories, and share homemade snacks. Sometimes they laughed so much their sides ached, and other times, they found themselves reminiscing about past adventures, adding new memories to their growing collection.

One of their favorite new traditions became Magic Hour, a time each day where Emma and Max would come together for a quiet activity. Sometimes they'd read, sometimes they'd work on a puzzle, and other times they'd simply sit outside, watching the world around them. They found that just being together, without any rush or distractions, made each day feel fuller.

Mrs. Baxter introduced a weekly "Gratitude Walk" on Sunday mornings. The family would walk through their neighbourhood or in the nearby park, each person taking turns sharing something they were grateful for that week. They pointed out small things—the warmth of the sun, the scent of flowers in bloom, the sound of birds chirping—that reminded them of the beauty in their lives.

Through each tradition, they practiced what Mr. Tockman had taught them: to slow down, to notice, and to be present. They didn't need grand adventures or special occasions to feel the magic of time;

they'd discovered that even the simplest moments could become precious memories.

One quiet evening, as they gathered in the backyard under the stars, Emma lay back and looked up at the twinkling sky. "Do you think we'll ever forget what Mr. Tockman taught us?" she asked, her voice soft.

Mr. Baxter shook his head, his eyes warm. "No, I don't think we ever could. He gave us a gift that's become a part of who we are. It's in the way we live now, in the way we take time to enjoy each other."

Max nodded, looking around at his family with a gentle smile. "We don't need a clock to make time feel special. We just need each other."

They sat together under the vast night sky, feeling the calm and peace of a day well spent. Each of them knew, without a doubt, that they would continue to carry the clockmaker's gift with them, creating a life filled with treasured moments.

As the stars twinkled above, they shared quiet dreams about the future, the adventures they hoped to have, and the memories they'd carry with them. They didn't feel the need to rush or stretch time; they had learned to let each moment unfold naturally, knowing that this was their own happily ever after.

And so, the Baxters continued to live their lives, savouring every day and cherishing every moment. They had learned to find magic in the simplest of things, to slow down and truly appreciate the gift of time.

In their own way, they were living happily ever after—slowed down, filled with love, and forever grateful for the time they shared together.

Disclaimer:

This book is a work of fiction, created for the enjoyment and inspiration of young readers and families. Any resemblance to actual persons, living or deceased, or to real events is purely coincidental.

The magical elements in this story, including the concept of slowing down time, are entirely fictional and intended to spark imagination and wonder. While the story highlights themes of family, mindfulness, and appreciating life's moments, readers are encouraged to interpret these themes in their own unique way.

Readers are also reminded that the use of clocks, watches, and other timekeeping devices in the story is part of a fictional narrative and does not represent real-life functionality or abilities.

Enjoy the journey, and remember that the true magic of time lies in cherishing each moment we share with those we love.